# The Secret at
# SUGAR SAND INN

## SUGAR SAND BEACH
## BOOK 2

# LEIGH DUNCAN

**The Secret at Sugar Sand Inn**
Sugar Sand Beach Series, Book #2

Copyright ©2021 by Leigh D. Duncan

This book is a work of fiction. The characters, events, and places portrayed in this book are products of the author's imagination and are either fictitious or are used fictitiously. Any similarity to real person, living or dead, is purely coincidental and not intended by the author.

Digital ISBN: 978-1-944258-26-9
Print ISBN: 978-1-944258-27-6
Gardenia Street Publishing

Published in the United States of America

Welcome Back to Sugar Sand Beach!

Escape to Sugar Sand Beach with Reggie Frank and her best friends for a second chance at all life has to offer.

Reggie has life all mapped out. The husband she put through law school has just landed his first big case. He'll probably make junior partner within the year. In no time at all, they'll move out of their cramped apartment, pay off the bills from the fertility clinic and buy a nice house in the suburbs, where they'll raise the baby Reggie longs to hold in her arms.

Except...life goes seriously off course when Reggie's husband walks out on their marriage the same day she receives the most devastating news. With her hopes and dreams for the future crumbling, Reggie turns to three of the best friends a girl could ever want. Helping them convert a run-down beach house into the Sugar Sand Inn is just the project Reggie needs to restore her self-confidence and heal her battered soul. A talented gardener, she volunteers to return the neglected grounds around the inn to their former glory with the help of handyman Chris Johnson.

In no time at all, Reggie's world is filled with bright possibilities for the home and family she's always wanted. But will the secret she harbors jeopardize Reggie's new-found happiness?

Join Reggie, Michelle, Nina and Erin as they build new lives in Sugar Sand Beach, where fresh opportunities for life, love and happiness are as limitless as the blue Florida skies.

# One

## Reggie

A solid thump jarred Reggie Frank out of a deep sleep. She blinked, struggling to get her bearings, trying to understand why her head pressed against something solid instead of the soft, fluffy pillow on her bed. A passing car honked, and everything came back in a rush. Sam had walked out on her, on their marriage. His leaving had pulled her life up by its roots, putting an end to her dreams of ever having a family, of having a baby of her own. With nothing to anchor her, she'd jumped at the chance to start a new life with her sister, Erin, and their two best friends, Michelle and Nina. Now, the four of them were on the final leg of their move from Virginia to Florida. The small trailer they towed behind her well-aged pickup held all Reggie's worldly belongings, plus a couple of plants wrapped in a waterproof tarp she'd secretly stashed back there. What hadn't fit in the trailer, she and Erin had crammed onto the crew cab's rear seat. In the Escalade behind them, Michelle and Nina pulled an even larger trailer, likewise filled to the brim with their own furniture and household goods.

"Where are we?" she asked, her voice still thick with sleep. She must have dozed off sitting in the passenger seat while Erin was driving. She yawned and stretched her arms.

"Welcome back, lazybones." Erin grinned without taking her eyes off the two-lane road that stretched into the distance. "We just passed through Crestview. Another hour, and we should be in Sugar Sand Beach."

Reggie grabbed the drink she'd picked up at their last pit stop. Condensation clung to the outside of the paper cup when she lifted it from the holder. A few pieces of ice sloshed against the sides. She sucked on the straw. The diluted soda only had two things going for it—it was wet and cold. For now, that was enough.

"It sure looks different down here." She eyed the passing scenery. As they'd traveled south, the hills of Virginia and North Carolina had flattened into a broad plain, broken only by the occasional overpass. Pine and pepper trees crowded against the barbed-wire fencing that lined both sides of the highway. Every once in a while, a break in the trees revealed grassy fields dotted with black and brown cows. "The trees are mostly evergreens. It's going to feel weird to go through the Fall without seeing the leaves change colors."

Erin shrugged. "Ah, but there are benefits. While everyone back home is bundling up, you'll be enjoying balmy ocean breezes and clear skies. And any time you want a taste of winter, you can always visit Mom and Dad." Their parents lived in a fifty-five-and-older community in West Virginia. "Personally, I'll take flip-flops and shorts over long johns and snow boots any day of the week."

"That does sound good," Reggie admitted. She trusted Erin to know what she was talking about. Her sister had wintered in the Florida Keys and summered in Alaska for the past twenty years. In between, she'd traveled the world, seeing everything from the Great Wall of China to the Inca ruins of Machu Picchu. "I have to admit, when you said you wanted to be a part of the inn, I nearly fell over. It's hard to imagine you staying in one place long enough to unpack your suitcase, much less put down roots." Even now, Erin traveled light. Her duffle bag and backpack hardly took up any room at all in the truck.

"I have enjoyed traveling. I won't deny it." Erin gave the blond hair she'd shoved into a ponytail a quick tug. "But the last couple of years, it didn't matter whether I was up in Seward or down in Islamorada, I've dreaded the end of the season. The thought of packing up and heading to my next gig just seemed like so much drudgery. I don't know if it's my age or what, but I'm looking forward to being in one place for a nice long while."

Was Erin slowing down because of her age? Would she, when she hit her forties? Not that she had to worry about that now. As the youngest of their tight-knit group of friends, she was only thirty-five. "I'll make sure one of the rocking chairs on the front porch has your name on it," Reggie quipped.

"Oh, puh-leez." Erin faked a groan.

"You want me to drive?" Her sister had taken the wheel when they stopped for gas south of Atlanta. That had been three hours ago.

"Nah. I'm good. Relax. You'll be busier than a one-armed paper hanger once we get there. We all will."

"Truth," Reggie acknowledged. "At least we have a place to sleep tonight. Cleaning out those rooms before we left was a smart move." On their first trip south to view the estate their friend Michelle had inherited from her birth mother, legal issues had delayed their return to Fairfax, the DC suburb they all called home. Michelle's new holdings were amazing—five acres with a beautiful Queen Anne-style house right on the beach in a sleepy little town between Destin and Panama City. The four of them had been friends for so long that it came as no surprise when they'd taken one look at the place and instantly decided to turn it into an inn.

When Michelle's lawyer insisted she stay over a few days to put the transfer of ownership in the works, they'd stuck by her side. But instead of hanging out at the beach and soaking up the sun's rays, each of them had cleaned one of the upstairs bedrooms. And, boy, had that been a job. The rambling, two-story house had been sitting vacant for five years and was in desperate need of mega doses of TLC. They'd had to scrub the rooms from top to bottom, beat the rugs and take down drapes that were so thick with dust, they sneezed just looking at them. But their hard work would pay off when they arrived this afternoon. They'd be able to move right into their temporary quarters, where they'd live while they renovated the rest of the house.

Not that they'd be tearing out walls or anything. The house was sound, the basics all in good shape, according to the inspector Michelle had hired. Still, between cleaning, painting and general all-around maintenance, they'd be hard-pressed to get the inn operational by Labor Day, when north Florida's winter tourist season kicked into high gear.

Erin cleared her throat. "I'm sure this is the right move for me. But, um…Are you sure it's the right move for you?"

"It's a little late to be asking that question now, don't you think?" Reggie aimed a thumb at the fully loaded trailer hitched to her pickup truck.

"I just…Well, there's no chance you and Sam will work things out?"

The mere mention of how fast her marriage of five years had fallen apart made Reggie's stomach ache. Less than a month ago, she'd been so certain the latest round of IVF treatments would work and she and Sam would finally have the family they'd longed for. Then came the devastating news that their fifth attempt at getting pregnant had been no more successful than the ones before it. That night, Sam hadn't even given her the chance to convince him they should give the expensive treatments one more try. He'd simply packed his bags and walked out. She hadn't heard from him since.

Well, she corrected, that wasn't quite true. Two days later, a courier had knocked on the door of their apartment. When she'd answered, the man in the black uniform had handed her a thin envelope containing the separation agreement Sam had oh-so-thoughtfully (not!) filled out. According to the note he'd attached, signing it would start a six-month countdown to the end of their marriage. A necessity according to Virginia law.

"I don't see how it's possible when we aren't speaking to each other. The only communication we have is through our lawyers. Thanks for making the appointment with Sheldon Cole, by the way." She paused. She'd always owe Erin for that. The minute Erin heard the man her baby sister had put through law school now intended to handle their divorce himself, Erin had insisted on hiring a divorce attorney to protect Reggie's interests. "He's opened my eyes to a couple of things."

"Such as?" Erin slowed as she steered onto a long, curving ramp that would take them east toward Destin.

"Well, for one, Sam offered to pay the rent on our apartment till the lease ran out. In exchange, he expected me to pay off our credit cards…and such." She caught herself before the fact slipped out that their debt included massive amounts of doctor bills and fertility treatments. Going through the divorce was tough enough without everyone finding out exactly why Sam had left her. Her face warmed just thinking about it. Raising a family was the whole purpose of getting married, yet she couldn't manage to get pregnant. No wonder Sam had called it quits.

She took another long sip from the nearly empty cup. She hadn't told anyone—not even Erin—about her fertility issues. She wasn't about to start now.

"But according to Mr. Cole," she said, sticking to the facts, "we incurred those debts as a couple, so they should be split fifty-fifty between us. Besides, hello! Now that I'm moving to Florida, I don't need or want the apartment. The attorney had me give him a list of everything Sam and I owned, right down to the number of towels in the linen closet. Then the two of them negotiated who got what. I ended up with the wide-screen TV; Sam took the stereo system. I got the weight set 'cause his salary at the law firm includes a gym membership. He took all the kitchen stuff, which I won't need at the inn. Et cetera. Et cetera."

"So, is it over then? You've signed the separation agreement?" Erin flipped her turn signal on. Speeding up at the end of the ramp, she merged in with the rest of the traffic.

"No." Reggie expelled a breath that carried more frustration than she liked. It took two people to make a marriage, and Sam's silence had made it clear he wasn't interested in reconciling. That positively broke her heart. But if there was no hope for a future with him, she couldn't wallow in the past. She'd seen too many women do that; it wasn't her style. She had to move on. Throwing in with Erin, Michelle and Nina on a new venture was a big part of her future. Finalizing things with Sam was another.

"I thought once we split up all our belong-ings, signing the agreement was the next step. But Mr. Cole said to hold off for now. He wants to take a closer look at our financials. I'm not sure why."

"Hmmm." Erin worried her lower lip the way she did whenever things troubled her. "He must suspect Sam's trying to cheat you somehow. This probably isn't any of my business, but wouldn't you know if something hinky was going on? All you'd have to do is check the bank balance, right?" Erin glanced in the side-view mirror as another car passed them.

"We don't have a joint checking account," Reggie admitted. She knew most married couples did, but Sam had begun handling the bills back when she was working two jobs to put him through law school. He'd continued keeping track of their finances even after he hired on at one of DC's most prestigious law firms. The few times she'd suggested letting her take on more responsibility for their household finances, he'd complained that changing the process wasn't worth the hassle. Instead, he figured out her share of the expenses each month. She paid it out of her meager earnings as a landscape assistant, and he took care of everything else.

Well, not quite everything, she corrected, thinking of the huge debt they'd racked up trying to have a baby.

"You really don't have any idea what Sam makes in a year, do you?" Erin took her eyes off the road just long enough to search Reggie's face.

"Well, no, but…" Reggie squirmed beneath her sister's pointed look. Not because she trusted Sam implicitly but because she'd had some of the same doubts herself. Until now, she'd tossed them aside like the fruitworms she removed from her tomato plants, but…

Suddenly uncomfortable, she crossed and re-crossed her legs. It was one thing for her to question Sam, but Erin's doubts put her on the defensive. Feeling like she needed to say something on her soon-to-be-ex-husband's behalf, she said, "Sam's always been fair. Last year, when I had the flu and couldn't work for three weeks, he covered the bills for the entire month." She grimaced. She'd meant to defend the man, but her protest fell flat, even in her own ears.

"It's okay. It's Mr. Cole's job to be cautious. That's all I'm saying." Erin's soothing words brought the tension in the car down a notch. "Chances are, he won't find anything to worry about."

Reggie thought Erin's tone said differently, but that was a topic to discuss another day, another time. For now, traffic had thickened to the point where it required her sister's full attention. More cars crowded the roadway as they approached the Choctawhatchee Bay that separated the mainland from the narrow peninsula that ran from east to west along the Gulf Coast. A sign up ahead announced the toll schedule for the Mid-Bay Bridge that would take them across the open water to Destin, and from there to their final destination in Sugar Sand Beach. Reggie scrounged in her purse for the eight-dollar fee, which she handed Erin when her sister pulled up to the toll booth.

"Welcome to Destin!" The clerk seated at the window smiled cheerily. "Aren't you brave, two girls like yourselves pulling a trailer like that. Where are y'all from?"

"Virginia," Erin answered briskly. At the end of the toll lane, the expected fee appeared on a screen.

"That'll be eight dollars. On account of the trailer," the woman drawled. "Y'all coming to stay or just passing through?" In a languid movement, she plucked the money from Erin's outstretched hand.

"We're moving to Sugar Sand Beach. Are you familiar with it?"

More accustomed to the unmanned toll booths in Virginia, Reggie felt her own eyebrows inch up her forehead while her sister and the clerk continued to chat as if there weren't twenty cars in line behind them.

"Pur-di-est beach around," the clerk declared. "I take my boys to swim there most weekends." She slipped the cash into a drawer and pressed a button. The screen up ahead went dark. Seconds later, a green light appeared.

"We're opening an inn there this fall," Erin announced. "Be sure to watch for it."

"Will do! Y'all take care now." The clerk waved goodbye.

Erin eased her foot off the brake, and the truck rolled forward. Checking the mirrors while she prepared to merge into the single lane that would take them onto the bridge, she said, "I can see now why traffic backs up at the toll booths. You think everyone down here is that friendly?"

"If they are, we'd better allow extra time to chat at the grocery store," Reggie answered with a grin. The suburbs of DC had long since assumed the same hustle and bustle as the big city. Florida's slower pace would take some getting used to.

"Is it my imagination, or is this a really long bridge?" Erin asked. She paced the vehicle in front of them, allowing a few car lengths between their bumpers. Oncoming traffic passed them in a steady stream.

"A little over three and a half miles." Not a fan of long bridges, Reggie stared through the passenger window while her stomach tightened. Beneath clear, blue skies, sunlight sparkled off water on either side of the bridge. She watched a distant sailboat skim across the surface. Other small craft bobbed at anchor or sped from one location to another, their motors humming. "I wouldn't want to cross the bay in bad weather." The waist-high guardrails looked sturdy enough when the sun was shining, but she could imagine how insubstantial they'd seem when the winds were blowing and rain was coming down in sheets.

"I did that once in the Keys. I was one of the last people across the Seven Mile Bridge after we were told to evacuate for a hurricane. Things got a little dicey, but at least the road was in good condition. Some of the bridges I've crossed in Bolivia and Brazil were real death traps."

"And yet you still went across them? Why?" Imagining her sister in danger, Reggie shifted toward the driver's seat. Though Erin often spoke of the wonderful sights she'd seen and the people she'd encountered in all her many travels, her sister rarely talked about the perils she'd faced.

"Most of the time, it was the only way to get where I wanted to go." Erin shrugged as if putting her life on the line hadn't mattered. "The Halsema Highway is considered one of the most dangerous roadways in the world, but in the Philippines, it's the best way to get to Sagada. The waterfalls and scenery there are too beautiful to miss. Definitely worth the risk."

Reggie wasn't so sure about that. She fidgeted in her seat until the car reached solid ground again and the uncomfortable tightness in her belly loosened. As far as she was concerned,

Erin could keep her bridges strung across gorges and mountain peaks. "I think I'd rather see the tulips in Holland or the rose gardens in Tuscany."

"You have to follow your own dreams, wherever they might lead," Erin said with a smile. "Right now, my dreams are taking me to a run-down house in Sugar Sand Beach."

"Don't worry. We'll get it whipped into shape in no time." Reggie stretched her legs into the foot well. She peered forward, eager for her first glimpse of the Gulf's calm waters as they turned onto Highway 98 and headed east toward Sugar Sand Beach.

At first, strip malls competed with tall condominiums to block the view. Those eventually gave way to sprawling time-share developments and residential communities where mature trees and gated entrances discouraged casual tourists from stopping.

"A girl could get used to this." Reggie sighed. She rolled down her window. Warm, moist air poured into the car. Savoring the fragrance of tropical plants and air that carried the slightest taste of salt, she licked her lips.

"It won't be long now."

For the next twenty minutes, Erin stayed in the right-hand lane of the four-lane highway.

Behind them, Michelle did the same, which let the faster-moving cars and trucks pass them on their eastbound journey. The road veered away from the beach, only occasionally swinging close enough to the shore for quick glimpses of the white, sandy beaches and gentle waves that lay beyond low bushes and palmetto. They were nearly to the Topsail Hill Preserve State Park, a 1600-acre nature preserve, when Erin slowed for a sharp turn onto a side street that cut through tall pines and scrub oak. A few more turns took them to a padlocked gate. Beyond it, twin rutted tracks disappeared over a slight hill.

"I'll get it." Reggie scrambled from the SUV, a copy of the key Michelle had given her clutched in her hand.

At the gate, she worked the key back and forth in the padlock a couple of times before the shackle popped open. Rusty metal complained loudly when she half-pushed, half-carried the simple swing gate through a drift of white sand mixed with gravel. Grinning, she doffed an imaginary hat and bowed with a flourish while Erin drove past and onto the lane. She bowed again when Michelle and Nina passed through a minute later. Reggie waited until the last trailer cleared the gate before she approached the second car.

"Do we want to lock up again?" she asked through Nina's open window.

Michelle leaned toward her. "Don't bother. I'm sure one of us will need to go out again later."

"Sounds good. I'll hang the padlock on the fence so it's there when we need it." Reggie slogged through the sand to the gate and slipped the lock through the hasp. Finished, she pocketed the key and returned to the pickup truck, which idled just in front of Michelle's big SUV.

"We're good to go," she said, slipping onto the passenger seat and pulling the door closed.

Slowly, Erin followed the rutted track up a gentle rise. As they topped the small hill, the house Michelle had inherited came into view. Erin took her foot off the gas and stared.

"Whoa. It sure looks different—better—now that we can see the windows."

Though the wrap-around porches, ginger-bread trim and a turret had created quite an impression on their last trip to Sugar Sand Beach, heavy metal shutters had covered every window and all but one of the doors like Band-Aids covered a child with chicken pox. But in the two weeks since they'd been here, someone—Reggie assumed it was the same handyman who'd performed essential tasks around the place for the past five years—had removed the storm shutters. Now, the sun's reflection sparkled in the dark panes of the windows on the porches on either side of the wide steps that led to the front door. The windows on the second floor caught more of the light.

"Wait," Reggie said, eyeing an odd glow from an upstairs window. "Is that stained glass up there?" She pointed to the balcony, where yellows, reds and greens danced in the sunlight.

Erin pulled her sunglasses down on her nose. Peering over them, she nodded. "We couldn't tell before with the windows all boarded up, but it sure looks like it."

"Cool," Reggie pronounced. Her pulse jumped. "I can't wait to see what the inside looks like now that we don't have to use flashlights." The first time they'd visited the house, they'd tried exploring by the light of their cell phones, but spiderwebs and the possibility of rotten floorboards had forced them to abandon ship. That evening, they'd stopped at a local home center, where they'd loaded up on flashlights and batteries. The next day, the added light had allowed them to move around freely, but they still hadn't seen into every nook and cranny.

Erin steered down the bumpy lane. As they neared the house, she pulled the car onto a weed-choked graveled pad, shifted into park, and shut off the engine. "Whew! I'm glad that part's over."

Michelle parked beside them a few seconds later. Practically at the same time, all four women spilled from their vehicles, eager to stretch their legs after the long trip.

"Oh! That feels good!" Her long, dark hair hanging loose, Nina clasped her hands over her head and repeatedly bent to touch her toes. "I was beginning to think we'd be in that car forever!"

"I can't believe we made it!" Michelle exclaimed. Hands on her hips, she twisted her torso back and forth a few times. "If I'd told Allen I planned to drive straight through from Virginia to Florida—pulling a trailer, no less— he'd have thought I'd lost my marbles."

Reggie froze in mid-stretch. It had only been a year since Michelle's husband of twenty-five years had suffered a sudden, fatal heart attack. Their friend still had moments when grief overwhelmed her. She waited to see if mentioning her late husband by name would trigger waterworks, but Michelle only paused for a second before she continued.

"And the kids all but threatened to have me committed. But we did it!" She patted Nina on the back. "I'm so proud of us." Her gaze landed first on Erin and then on Reggie. "Of all of us!"

"We've accomplished a lot in just two weeks," Nina agreed. "I quit my job, gave up my apartment, packed up everything I wanted and got rid of the rest."

"Whew! So much has happened, I don't even know where to begin," Reggie said when the conversational ball landed in her court. She held up one hand and began ticking off items on her fingers. "I'm pretty much in the same boat as Nina, except I lost a husband somewhere along the way."

"No big loss," Nina muttered.

Reggie's neck stiffened, and she pouted. "That wasn't very nice."

"You're my friend, and you deserve better. That's all I'm saying," Nina countered.

If Nina and the others only knew the truth, they wouldn't be so quick to take her side, Reggie thought. She wasn't a doctor or a college professor like some of the wives of the other attorneys at Sam's firm. She hadn't joined the Junior Women's League, and she was too busy earning a living to spend her days organizing fundraisers for one charitable cause after another. When she came home after work, she often smelled like the manure she'd spent the day shoveling around flower beds, a fact her lawyer husband frequently pointed out to her. Plus, after years of trying every trick in the book to have a baby, she'd failed. The plain truth was, she didn't measure up. No wonder Sam had moved on with his life.

When Reggie fell silent, Erin stepped in. "I'll say one thing about Sam, and that's that he was smart enough to marry my sister but not smart enough to hang on to her. But don't worry, Reggie. You have us to make up for his loss."

Though Reggie's face burned with shame, she was grateful for her sister's support. She was even more thankful when Erin deftly steered the conversation in another direction.

Erin pointed to the slim, dark-haired widow. "Chelle's the one I'm in awe of. She sold her house, packed up all her belongings, held a *massive* yard sale—"

"The best one Fairfax has ever seen," Michelle put in.

"You're right about that." A yoga enthusiast, Nina shifted into a side oblique stretch. "I think the people who bought your dining-room set are still asking themselves when you're going to track them down and tell them it was all a big joke and you want your table and chairs back."

"I did give them a pretty good deal on it,"

Michelle admitted. She tucked a strand of glossy black, chin-length hair behind her ear.

"Are you kidding? They made out like bandits," Reggie gushed. There'd been a time when she'd practically coveted the rosewood table and chairs.

"Well, I couldn't have done it all without your help. Especially Erin's." Michelle gave the tall, rangy blonde a quick squeeze. "I don't know what I would have done if she hadn't been there, cracking the whip every day."

Had it only been a month ago that Erin had flown in from who-knew-where and the four of them had gathered in Michelle's den to comfort their friend on the anniversary of her husband's death? It seemed impossible that such a short time had passed since Michelle had confessed that the precarious state of her finances was forcing her to sell the beautiful Colonial where she and Allen had raised their family. They'd all barely gotten over that news when Michelle learned her birth mother, a woman she'd never met, had left everything she owned to the child she'd put up for adoption forty-five years earlier. As Nancy Simmons's sole heir, Michelle had inherited a gorgeous Queen Anne-style house along with five acres of Gulf-front property in Sugar Sand Beach. Acting on a spur-of-the-moment decision, the four of them had pooled their resources to pay the taxes on the place and had spent the last two weeks preparing for the move to Florida, where, over the next several months, they intended to convert the house into an inn.

Some had questioned their decision. In their junior year at the University of Virginia, Michelle's twins, Ashley and Aaron, certainly hadn't been in favor of their mother's plans. Neither had Sam, not that what Reggie did or didn't do was any of his business. Not anymore. But Reggie and the others had high hopes they could make their dream come true. Nina was a world-class chef. With her skills in the kitchen, the café she planned to open was certain to be a huge success. Michelle had more decorating talent in her little finger than most women had in their entire bodies. And if that wasn't enough, her years of hosting everything from birthday parties to anniversary dinners to the launch of her husband's business had given her the skills of a consummate hostess. She'd do an awesome job of handling reservations and making their guests feel right at home. Erin had spent over twenty years touring the globe. An avid kayaker, she'd take charge of providing tours and outdoor activities.

As for herself, she loved working outside, digging around in the dirt, caring for plants and watching them blossom. Her experience working in some of the best nurseries and with the best landscapers in the DC area would come in handy here at the inn. Her first task would be to clear out the plants that had grown wild in the five years the house had been sitting vacant. By nurturing the bushes and shrubs that had suffered from neglect, she'd restore the outside to its original beauty. She'd also create paths for their guests to wander near the lake out back and down to the beach in the front. And then there was the garden. She had big plans for that. This one would eventually provide fresh fruits and vegetables for Nina's café. Michelle would use her flowers in bouquets and wreaths throughout the inn.

Yep. No doubt about it. They could do this. With the four of them working together, they could take the property and house Michelle had inherited and turn it into a place people would never want to leave. And there was no time like the present to get started. Eagerly, she rubbed her hands together just as Michelle jingled a set of keys.

"Well, those trailers won't empty themselves. What say we take a quick look around and then get them unloaded." Keys in hand, Michelle skipped up the stairs to the front door.

While the others surged toward the steps, Nina hung back. "I should get Mr. Pibbs out of his cat carrier. Poor baby. I bet he's as glad as the rest of us to be here. I'm going to keep him in my room for the time being…until he gets used to the place. Is that okay with everyone?"

Though none of the others had pets, they'd all agreed that Mr. Pibbs was as much a part of the family as Michelle's twins.

"I'll help," Reggie offered, turning. "What do you need besides his carrier?"

"Nah, I got it," Nina insisted. "He's going to be in a mood after being cooped up so long. I have everything he needs in a tote bag behind the front seat. I'll just run him upstairs, set up his litter box and let him get settled. You go on with the others. I'll catch up in a few minutes."

While Nina grabbed the cat carrier and a tote bag, Reggie and Erin joined Michelle at the front door. Reggie braced for furnace-like temperatures and held her breath when Michelle pushed the door open. Inside, however, heavy drapes over the windows had blocked the sunlight. The added insulation had kept the house surprisingly cool.

"Maybe we should have brought the flashlights," Michelle murmured. Thin shafts of light filtered between the gaps in the draperies. Beyond the bright spots, the room dissolved into shadows.

"I know how to fix that," Erin declared. Crossing to the nearest set of tall windows, she pushed aside the drapes, located a pair of ornate tiebacks mounted on the walls and clamped window coverings in place.

The effect was as immediate as it was stunning. All the colors in a box of crayons danced across the walls and hardwood floors when light struck the hundreds of drops that hung from an immense chandelier. The darkness receded, giving them their first good look at deep crown moldings that circled the hammered tin ceiling, the whitewashed mantel over the fireplace. Drop cloths draped a half dozen couches and chairs. Reggie lifted one sheet to peer beneath. She quickly dropped it back in place when five years' worth of dust and grime threatened to spill onto the hardwood floor. More dust floated thickly in the wide rays of sunlight that streamed through the windows.

"I hope someone brought a vacuum," she said. "I'm going to check out that stained-glass window we saw on our way up the drive."

Leaving Erin and Michelle to explore the first level, she climbed the curving staircase to the second floor. Rather than the near pitch-blackness of the downstairs, light filtered through a large stained-glass window overlooking a balcony at the end of the wide hallway. Reggie's breath caught in her throat as she studied the image wrought in the glass. The tall Grecian urn filled with thin green leaves and cattails was a thing of beauty.

"Wow," she whispered, imagining herself sipping from a cup of coffee while sitting at a nearby table. She moved closer, hoping for a better look, but retreated when she spotted spiderwebs stretched across the colored glass panes. "Another time," she promised.

Before heading downstairs, she popped her head into the bedroom she'd chosen for her temporary quarters. Here, a large oak dresser and a tall chest of drawers flanked a queen-size bed. Tall casement windows hid behind floor-to-ceiling drapes. In the light that streamed through the thick glass panes once she'd opened the curtains, she saw a light coating of dust on the floors. Other than that, though, everything was exactly as she'd left it two weeks ago. An attached sitting room sat vacant, the perfect place for the few pieces of living-room furniture she'd brought with her from Virginia.

She returned to the hall at the same time Nina

was quickly exiting her own suite. The taller woman closed the door behind her.

"How's Mr. Pibbs like his new digs?" Reggie asked.

Nina held up a pair of crossed fingers. "So far, so good. When I left, he was patrolling the bathroom. Like it was his job to make sure I'm safe from any intruders."

"Let's hope he doesn't find any," Reggie quipped as they headed downstairs to find Michelle and Erin. Not spotting anyone in the front parlor, she called, "Hey, everybody. Wait till you see the stained-glass window over the balcony. It's so pretty."

From another part of the house, her sister called out. "There's another one in the back parlor. Some kind of tall vase."

"And cattails?" Reggie followed the sound of her sister's voice. She found Erin standing with her hands on her hips, studying hundreds of books that lined the shelves of the library.

"Yeah. I think so."

"Stained-glass windows and a fully stocked library." Reggie whistled. "What a nice surprise."

"I imagine we're going to stumble across quite a few surprises as we go through the house," Michelle said, joining them. "In fact, I just found a big one." She crossed to a nearby wall switch and flipped it. Light blazed into the room from a globe attached to an overhead ceiling fan.

"You're kidding. The electricity's on?" Reggie's mouth dropped open. The last time they'd visited the house, the power had been turned off. She'd assumed it still would be. Evidently, she wasn't the only one who'd jumped to that conclusion. She glanced at the others. Surprise registered on their faces, too.

"Does that mean we have air-conditioning?" Erin asked.

"Are the refrigerator and freezer operational?" Nina asked. "It'd be nice if we didn't have to lug in ice from the convenience store."

Michelle held up one hand. "Those are all things we'll have to figure out. For now, what say we start bringing in our stuff. I'd like to return my trailer to the rental place first thing tomorrow."

"Sounds good to me," Reggie nodded. She was on a shoestring budget until they got the inn up and running. If she could avoid another day's rental, she'd just as soon save the money for something else. Besides, she needed to get those plants out of the trailer ASAP.

"I thought I'd order in pizza for dinner tonight, if that sounds good to everyone," Nina put in. "I want to make sure the appliances are in good working order before I lay in a supply of groceries."

"Pizza's fine," Erin agreed for all of them. "We can take a short break to eat and then work as long as we want."

Michelle frowned. "I was hoping we could put our heads together and come up with a name for this place sometime soon. We were thinking about Sugar Sand Inn earlier, but don't you think that's just a little too simple?"

"It could be. But making that decision sounds like something we ought to do over a bottle of wine," said Nina.

"Or two," added Erin.

"Okay, let's do this. We'll unload, unpack as much as we can, and meet downstairs for pizza at six. We can talk about our plans for the week and figure out what we want to call the inn after dinner. Then whoever wants to go back to work can do that."

Reggie rubbed her hands together. For a while there, she'd thought all her dreams for the future had died when Sam walked out on her. But her friends and her sister had given her a new purpose, a second chance. She couldn't wait to get started on her new life in Sugar Sand Beach.

# Two

## Michelle

Sitting at the breakfast nook, Michelle Robinson flexed her arms and tried unsuccessfully to work the soreness out of her shoulders. Long hours behind the wheel of the car, followed by too much heavy lifting and toting as she and Nina had unloaded the trailer, hadn't done her forty-five-year-old, slightly out of shape body any favors. She felt like she could use good soak in a tub full of Bengay. Except the last thing anyone in the house wanted was the smell of all that menthol floating in the still air. Even with the windows open, it'd take days for the odor to go away. No, a glass of wine and a heating pad would work nearly as well. She'd settle down for a nice long session with both before she turned in for the night.

Looking around the table, she wondered if her friends were feeling the same sort of aches and pains. But judging from their easy banter as they scarfed down pizza, apparently not. At thirty-five, Reggie not only had youth on her side, her job in landscaping helped keep her compact body well-toned. Across from her sat Erin, a woman who ran 5Ks for fun and thought nothing of trekking across the Sahara or going on safari in Africa. She certainly wasn't feeling any ill effects from the move. Last, but certainly not least, came Nina. Long and lean, she moved with the grace of a prima ballerina. No one looking at her would think she regularly spent ten or twelve hours a day as a chef in one of the busiest—and best—kitchens in the DC area. Michelle gave her head a slight shake. If she worked around all that delectable food day in and day out, she'd carry far more than fifteen extra pounds on her frame. Why, she'd be as round as a cantaloupe.

Determined to start her diet tomorrow, she grabbed a second slice of pizza. Though the crust was doughy and the pepperoni had been sliced paper-thin, the marinara had a nice tang to it. "This isn't half bad," she said, taking a bite. "Where'd you say you got it?"

"Maggie's Diner," Nina answered. She and

Reggie had picked up takeout after learning no one nearby delivered. "As near as I can tell, it's the only place that serves food for miles around."

"Sounds like the area needs a great little café," Reggie remarked. "Here's to Nina's." She lifted her glass of wine in a toast.

"That's not going to be for a while," Nina said. "I need to check in with the local Health Department—I'm sure I'll need a separate business license from the inn's. And that's after I scrub every inch of the kitchen, check out all the appliances, make sure everything's in order. The list goes on." She dabbed a bit of grease from her lips with a paper napkin.

"I can lend a hand with the cleaning," Erin offered. "I'm sure we'll all get tired of takeout from Maggie's pretty quick. After that, I'd like get those kayaks down out of the garage and see if they'll float." On their first trip to Sugar Sand Beach, they'd discovered all manner of vehicles and watercraft stored in the garage, but there hadn't been time for more than a cursory look at them.

"How about you, Reggie? What's on your agenda?" Michelle turned to the petite strawberry blonde who'd agreed to take charge of the exterior.

"There's so much work to do, it's hard to

know where to start," Reggie admitted. "I think the first thing will be to get the tractor up and running. Using it will make clearing the overgrowth a lot easier and quicker than doing it by hand. I'd like to get started on the garden as soon as possible so that, by the time Nina's ready to open the café, we can use some of our own produce. Before that, though, I need to visit some of the local nurseries. I think I have a handle on what grows in this climate, but it's always good to get advice from people who actually live here." She scrunched her napkin into a ball. "How about you? What's at the top of your list?"

"If he's available, I need to go into Destin tomorrow and see Dave Rollins." The attorney had handled her birth mother's estate and had been instrumental in identifying her as Nancy Simmons's sole heir. "In his last email, he said he had the final paperwork for the transfer of ownership ready to sign. I'm sure he's the one we have to thank for getting the utilities turned on, too. I'll need to switch those accounts into my name."

"Or the inn's," Erin suggested.

Michelle cupped her chin in one hand. "It's too soon to do that now, but once we have a business license, I'm sure we'll have to set up business accounts. And"—she circled one finger in the air—"that brings us to what we're going to call this venture of ours. Any ideas?" She surveyed the table.

Erin cleared her throat. "I've researched the area a good bit since our last trip here. The usual big chain resorts and inns—with names we'd all recognize—are mostly in Destin or farther east along the coast, closer to Panama City. Around here, there's a smattering of Airbnbs that, near as I could tell, operate from October to March each year. I might be wrong—there could be something I've missed—but I couldn't find anything like what we're proposing within thirty miles. As for names, there's a Gulfside Inn up the coast a bit."

"How about the Choctawhatchee Bay Inn?" Reggie suggested. She groaned. "Scratch that. It doesn't exactly roll off the tongue, does it?"

"Not exactly," Michelle agreed. She emptied the last few drips of wine into Erin's glass and opened another bottle.

"Maybe Seaside Inn?" Reggie suggested, trying again.

"Eh, we're not really so much on the sea as we are on the Gulf," Nina pointed out.

"What about Fun and Sun Inn?" Michelle asked as she topped off everyone's glasses.

"We have such a great location. I think people

should be able to tell we're on the beach when they see the name," Erin mused.

"That makes sense," Michelle agreed. Around the table, heads bobbed.

"What else is nearby?" Nina swirled the red wine in her glass. "Maybe we could name it after a local historical site?"

"Well, Destin used to claim to have the World's Largest Fishing Lure, but I think Fishing Lure Inn would attract a different kind of customer than the couples or young families we're hoping for."

Mirth danced in Reggie's eyes. "This is getting complicated. Whenever we had a customer come into the nursery with plans for a complicated landscape, my boss would say they needed to employ the KISS principle."

Michelle's eyebrows knitted. "What's that?"

Reggie's full lips slanted into a teasing smile. "Keep it simple, stupid."

"Oh! That's a hoot." Nina chortled while everyone else laughed.

"But she has a point," Erin said when the last of the chuckles faded. "Maybe we shouldn't get too carried away trying to be creative. Look, in deciding not to sell, we're preserving the essence of Sugar Sand Beach, right?"

"Right," Michelle nodded. According to Dave

Rollins, a local real estate agent by the name of Oscar Danner had hoped to buy the Simmons property for a group of Northern businessmen who'd decided Sugar Sand Beach was prime for development. Their plans to erect a hundred or more tiny houses sitting cheek-to-jowl on what was now Michelle's five acres would have destroyed the atmosphere of the laid-back little community.

"Why not stick with a name that reflects our ties to the area then?" Erin asked.

Michelle took a fortifying sip of wine. "You mean Sugar Sand Inn?" Personally, she loved the idea and wondered why she'd ever wanted to change it. She held her breath while the others gave the matter some thought.

The first to react, Reggie slapped her hand on the tabletop. "I like it!"

"It definitely lets people know where we're located," Nina said, weighing in a few seconds later.

"And it tells them a little bit about the place— that it's known for beaches with sand as fine as sugar," Erin added. She raised her glass. "I think we have a keeper. Here's to Sugar Sand Inn!"

"Here, here," Michelle said, clinking her glass against the others.

While Nina and Erin sipped their wine,

Reggie drained her glass in a couple of gulps. "I don't know about the rest of you, but between the drive down here and unloading the trailer, I'm bushed," she announced. She rose, walked around the wide center aisle and set her glass in the sink.

Nina pressed her shoulders back, her elbows bent, fingers curled inward. "I could sleep," she admitted.

Erin didn't quite yawn, but it sure looked like she was dead on her feet. Trying her best not to wince, Michelle pushed up from the table. "Let's call it a night. We have a busy day tomorrow."

"The first of many," Erin said. She stacked their used paper plates on top of one another. "Where do we put the trash?" she asked no one in particular.

"I brought garbage bags." Nina pulled one from a box under the counter and held it open.

Michelle tossed in the empty pizza box. "Guess we'll need to figure out the local trash pickup dates and the ins and outs of the recycling program."

"I'll poke around tomorrow, see if Nancy had a compost bin anywhere. If she didn't, do you think we should start one?" Reggie rubbed sleep from her eyes.

"It's your call, Reg." Still holding the trash

bag, Erin nudged her sister with one elbow. "You're in charge of all that outside stuff."

"Really?" Reggie's eyes widened a bit. Slowly, she turned to Michelle. "I'm not used to making a lot of big decisions on my own. Little ones, either. Sam felt, as the man of the house, it was his job to decide everything from where we went on vacation to what we had for dinner." As if realizing she'd said more than she'd intended, she scuffed one toe against the floor. "You, uh, you don't want me to run everything past you?"

"No, hon." Michelle smiled softly. "First off, I'm not in charge. We're all in this together. My name might be on the deed—or it will be once I sign the papers Dave has for me—but this is definitely a joint effort. You just let one of us know when you run into trouble or feel like you need a second opinion." She looked to the others for confirmation and saw only support in their expressions. "We'll all do the same. That sound like something you can work with?"

A slow smile slid across Reggie's lips. She expelled a breath. "I like the sound of that. And now, for my first executive decision, I'm going to take this tired girl to bed."

"Likewise," Nina said. "I suspect Mr. Pibbs is going to want some cuddle time."

"Give him some love for me," Michelle said.

"You going up?" Erin asked as she passed.

"In a little bit," Michelle answered.

Erin stayed put a moment longer. "Thanks for that last bit with Reggie. She's struggling with the whole divorce thing. I think it might take her a while to get out from under Sam's thumb and stand on her own two feet. But, with a little help from people who love her, she'll do it."

"We're all here for her—especially you. You're a good sister. She's lucky to have you." Michelle gave her friend a hug.

She watched as Erin trailed the others up the stairs. She lingered until floorboards creaked overhead. Doors closed, and the house grew quiet again.

Erin was right, Michelle thought as she emptied the last of the wine into her glass. She was going to enjoy watching Reggie come out of her shell, learn to trust her own strengths, figure out her weaknesses and when she needed to turn to the others for help. She'd seen Reggie falter when she started to unload the trailer earlier. Small wonder. A few odds and ends weren't much to show for the years she'd invested in Sam. Personally, she'd never seen what Reggie liked in the guy. He'd always come across as too full of himself. And the way he'd expected Reggie to kowtow to his every demand had raised the hackles on the back of her neck on more than one occasion. In her opinion, Reggie was better off without him. But, then again, who was she to judge? Lord knew, she and Allen had had their ups and downs. Not that he'd tried to control her or keep her under his thumb. If he had, she'd have given him what for from the get go.

No, their problems had, strangely enough, centered on his eternal optimism. Most people considered that a good trait, but she'd learned differently. The problem with someone who never saw the down side of things was that they didn't plan for the possibility of things going sideways. Allen sure hadn't. Only someone who always saw the upside, who never even imagined things might not go according to his plan, would fail to carry adequate life insurance. Or would borrow so heavily on the equity in their house that, when the unthinkable did happen, their surviving spouse would be forced to choose between selling it or letting the bank foreclose.

She took a deep breath and deliberately counted down from ten. What had happened with Allen was water under the bridge. She would not, could not dwell on the man's faults. That way led to bitterness, and she certainly wasn't going to wallow in that nastiness.

Instead, she'd follow the advice of the counselor for the grief group at the Y and focus on the positives. She held out one hand and began ticking items off. She and Allen had enjoyed twenty-five years together. They'd been blessed with two healthy babies, which they'd raised into young adulthood. They'd developed friendships, traveled, enjoyed the time God had given them. She'd never thought she'd be embarking on a whole new life at forty-five, but at least she wasn't doing it alone. She had three of the best friends anyone could ever ask for at her side. Together, they'd turn the property her birth mother had left her into a first-class inn and build new lives for themselves here in Sugar Sand Beach.

By the time she finished with her list, she felt more at ease with herself. She checked the doors a final time and turned out the lights. Standing at the base of the stairs holding a half-full glass of wine in one hand, she paused, listening. Beyond the windows, cicadas buzzed. An owl hooted from somewhere nearby. Above her head, the creak of a floorboard sent chills racing down her arms. In the quarter of a century that had passed since she'd picked up lock, stock and barrel and moved, she'd nearly forgotten how strange it felt to be in an unfamiliar place.

Houses always felt strange at first, she reminded herself. She'd get used to this one in time. Maybe not tonight, but that was okay. She had something else to take care of before she turned in.

Ever since he'd handed it to her, she'd been waiting for the right opportunity to open the letter Dave Rollins had given her. The one her birth mother had written. She supposed she could have read it that day on the beach. As much as she thought he was a nice guy, though, she hadn't wanted Dave looking at her, watching her, as she read a note from the woman who'd given her life and then given her away. Once she got back to Virginia, she hadn't had a spare moment. Her life had turned into a whirlwind of transferring bank accounts, dealing with the twins, choosing which of their many possessions to keep and what to dispose of, saying goodbye to neighbors and friends. She'd loaded the trailer and headed south two days after that massive yard sale—no one could have expected her to read the letter while she was behind the wheel.

So, here she was, in Nancy Simmons's house. Thinking about the letter Dave Rollins had given her, the one that rested in the still-sealed envelope tucked into the bottom of her purse.

The time had come. She took the stairs one at a time, trying not to wince or spill her wine with every step. It seemed fitting somehow that tonight she'd finally read the letter her mother had given her.

# Three

## Erin

In the upstairs bedroom she'd chosen for her temporary quarters, Erin finished working through her daily regimen of limbering stretches. She shook her arms out, relieving the tightness of bunched muscles that had gone too long without a full workout. While she definitely hadn't lazed about eating bonbons and catching up on all the soaps this past month, she hadn't exactly been to the gym. Or been on the right side of a boat in far too long. Boxing up Michelle's possessions, loading them into the trailer, unloading them on the other end kept her busy, but she yearned for the dip and push of her paddle as she cut through the water, for the lapping sound the ripples made against the sides of her kayak, for the rush of the wind against her face. As soon as possible, she'd get those old boats down out of the garage and take them for a test spin.

And if they didn't float after being in storage for a decade or two? Well, she had two top-of-the-line kayaks just sitting at her cottage in the Keys. She'd run down there one weekend and haul them up here.

But not today. Today, on their first full day in Sugar Sand Beach, she'd promised to help Nina in the kitchen. If she had time, she'd assemble Reggie's gym equipment in a spare room so they'd all have a place to work out later. But first, coffee.

Reaching into her duffle, she unearthed the simple, drip-style cone she carried with her on her travels about the globe. With it and a tablespoon of grounds, she could brew herself a cup of java wherever she had water. It might not make the best coffee in the world—for that she'd need a French press and a pound of Tanzanian Peaberry—but it would do in a pinch.

Nothing stirred when she eased her bedroom door open a few minutes later. Not that she was a bit surprised. After the long drive yesterday, she, Nina, Reggie and Michelle had spent several hours unloading the trailers. Then they'd stayed up late, talking and laughing until well past midnight. Guided by the first rays of morning light that sifted through the stained-glass window at the end of the hall, Erin padded down the stairs on bare feet. Halfway to the kitchen, where she hoped she could figure out how to boil water on the big Aga cook stove, she caught the faint scent of coffee and smiled. Someone had beaten her out of bed this morning after all.

Walking into the spacious kitchen, she spotted a Keurig sitting on the counter, all plugged in and ready to go. Not one to turn her nose up at the convenience of a freshly brewed cup, Erin sat her ceramic filter aside. She mumbled a quick "Hey" to Michelle, who had tucked herself into the corner of the breakfast nook. "Mind if I have a cup?"

"Help yourself." Michelle answered without looking up. "I'm sorry there's no creamer or sugar. I didn't think to bring them."

"No problem. I've gotten used to drinking it black over the years." After all, it wasn't like she could just pop into a corner market to pick some up while trekking through the wilds of Kenya.

"Yeah, but…I sure wish I had some."

Erin went on alert. Michelle's voice held a note of sadness that went far deeper than a wistful yearning for condiments. Leaving the coffee gurgling into her cup, she took a good, long look at her friend. She'd assumed, from Michelle's hunched posture, that the brunette was taking care of email and such, but her phone sat face-down on the kitchen table. She looked smaller and far older than a mere forty-five. Her red-rimmed eyes testified to a sleepless night.

Erin stifled a groan. She hadn't seen her friend looking this low since the days immediately following Allen's death. Her quest for coffee forgotten, she crossed the room and slid onto the bench. "What's wrong, Chelle?" Her heart skipped a beat. "Are the kids okay?"

"No, they're fine. At least, I think they are. I'm not exactly their most favorite person right now, you know?" Michelle managed a wavery smile.

Erin clenched her teeth. Clearly, she was going to have to have a heart-to-heart with Ashley and Aaron. It was high time her godchildren ditched the diapers and the whiny attitudes, pulled up their big-girl and big-boy panties and started acting like young adults. Not that their problems with their mother were all one-sided. She seriously doubted Michelle had been as straightforward as she could have been about the financial mess Allen had left her in. She understood that. Michelle was their mother, after all, and she wanted to preserve the good memories her children had of their father. Erin, however, didn't operate under the same constraints. Sooner, rather than later, she'd clarify things for the twins, if only so they'd pull together to support their mom. But that was a task for another day. Right now, she needed to get to the bottom of Michelle's problems.

"So, if my lovely godchildren haven't got you down in the dumps, what does?"

"This." Michelle reached into the pocket of her robe and pulled out several pieces of folded paper.

"A letter?" Erin's brow furrowed. "Who from?"

"Nancy Simmons."

"Your birth mother." Erin nodded. Less than a month had passed since a private investigator had tracked down Michelle and delivered the news that her birth mother had died and left all her worldly goods to her only child. She traced her fingers over the sheets of thick, personal stationery. Lines of neat cursive filled several pages. "Can I?" At Michelle's nod, she scooped up the letter. "Where'd you get this?" she asked while she skimmed the first few lines.

"Dave handed the envelope to me that day he told us the news about the lab results."

"At the beach, you mean?" The lawyer handling Nancy Simmons's estate had shown up at their picnic to personally deliver the news that DNA tests had confirmed Michelle's relationship to his client.

"Yes."

"Whew." Erin let out a long, slow breath. "That was weeks ago. You're just now opening it?"

Michelle steepled her hands with her thumbs under her chin. "I knew I'd need some time to think about it, no matter what she'd written. But with all the other stuff that was going on—deciding whether to keep this property or sell it, figuring out what to do about my house, dealing with the kids—I didn't have that kind of time, so I put it off. Besides, I figured she had to be looking for forgiveness. Right?"

"Was she?" Erin waited expectantly.

"Not exactly. I've been up all night, and I still don't know what to think of it all."

"What's it say?" Erin slid the note across the table to Michelle. They might be close as sisters, but that didn't give her the right to take more than a cursory look at a letter from her birth mother.

"It's all incredibly sad." Michelle shuddered a breath. "She was eighteen and in love." She tapped the paper. "Nancy never mentions his name. Just that he'd been drafted into the army. Vietnam," she said with a sigh. "He proposed the

50

night before he shipped out and they, well…she got pregnant. She hid the news for six months before she broke down and told her parents."

"I bet that didn't go over well. Single parenting is a lot more acceptable now, but in the seventies?" Erin shook her head.

"It didn't. Her parents were devastated and angry in equal measure. They insisted she spend the rest of the pregnancy at a home for unwed mothers. They told everyone they were going to a Christmas pageant, but really, they were planning to drop Nancy off on the night of the accident. She doesn't go into details, but I bet you could cut the tension in the car that night with a knife. Throw in a thunderstorm, and it'd be easy for someone to lose their focus and miss a curve."

"And that's what happened?" Erin prompted.

Michelle nodded. "She woke up in the hospital unable to walk. Both her parents had died in the crash. It nearly destroyed her. She writes that the baby she carried was only thing that kept her going. But then she received news that her fiancé had died in Vietnam."

The loss punched Erin in the gut. She hissed. "Tragic."

"According to her letter, she said that's when she knew she couldn't keep her baby. Along with her ability to walk, her independence, she'd lost everyone she loved. At eighteen, it had to be overwhelming. All she could see was a life of sadness and pain. She wanted better than that for her child. For me. So she contacted an adoption agency run by the Lutheran church. The rest, as they say, is history." Michelle stacked the pages, one on top of the other, and folded them in half.

"Except."

"You knew there was more to it than that, didn't you?" Michelle's thin lips formed a wan smile. She took a breath. "There was. A couple of years later, once the shock of losing her parents and her fiancé had worn off, Nancy tried to find her child. Not to take the baby back—she said she wouldn't do that to the adoptive parents. But she wanted some reassurance that she'd made the right decision, that she'd given her child— given me—a chance at happiness."

"I take it that didn't go as well as she'd hoped?" Michelle had tried on numerous occasions to locate her birth parents. But Florida's adoption laws were some of the most restrictive in the nation. Her efforts had invariably hit a brick wall.

"No. She was eighteen—or maybe nineteen— when she had me. Younger than Ashley is now. It probably didn't sink in that her connection to her child would be permanently severed once she signed the papers. She said leaving me her estate wasn't a plea for forgiveness as much as it was the only way she had of making sure I ended up with the kind of life she wanted for me."

"Wow!" Erin finger-combed her hair. "That's a lot to take in. No wonder your eyes are, well, red." She took a closer look at her friend. "Did you get *any* sleep last night?"

"Not really." Michelle's lips thinned. "I kept thinking of how much loss Nancy suffered. Her parents. Her fiancé. Her child. Plus, she lost the ability to walk. So much tragedy for one person to endure. I can't help asking how one person sustained all that and still…" Her voice faltered.

Erin reached for her friend's hand. "And still what, Chelle? Carried on?" She wasn't certain she'd be up to that challenge.

"Not just carried on but excelled. I mean, look at all the contributions she made. All those boards and committees she served on. All the money she donated to the community. People around here think she walked on water." Michelle giggled and clamped one hand over her mouth. "Pardon the pun."

"Oh, that's funny."

"That's exhaustion. That's what it is."

Michelle stretched. "Whatever. Nancy's letter has forced me to take a good, hard look at my own life. I lost Allen and with him, our life's savings. My kids and I are on the outs. Even though I know they'll come around eventually, it still hurts enough that I've wallowed in self-pity more than I like to admit."

"Who wouldn't?" Erin asked. Personally, she thought Michelle had handled her grief far better than she would under the same circumstances.

"But after reading this"—Michelle tapped the folded stationery—"after learning all Nancy went through and that she still gave so much to her community, I have to stop and ask myself, how could I dare give up? It's made me see how important it is that we move forward with the inn, with making it a success. Not just for me, but for all of us. So we have a stake in something bigger than ourselves."

"That's awfully deep for someone who hasn't had her first cup of coffee yet." Erin glanced at the Keurig, where her own mug sat cooling.

Michelle gave a rueful grin as she lifted an empty cup. "Speak for yourself. I've been mainlining the stuff since two."

"Sounds like you're ready for a refill." She took Michelle's cup to the pot and quickly filled it. Her own coffee had grown cold while they'd talked, but she grabbed it anyway. Her years of constant travel had taught her the value of making do. She took a long swallow and nearly convinced herself she enjoyed it.

"You still going into Destin this morning?" Erin asked when she'd set both cups on the table.

"I have to. I texted Dave last night before I went to bed. He has some free time around nine."

Beyond the kitchen windows, sunlight played on tall sea oats that tossed to and fro in the breeze. A stork with stilt-like legs moved slowly across the backyard. He stopped occasionally to peck for his breakfast in the grass. "You'd better get a move on then," she said.

Michelle lifted her cell phone from the table and turned it over to check the time. "Ooops. It's later than I thought. I don't want to keep the man waiting."

Erin tapped her chin. According to what the attorney had told them when they first met, Dave Rollins had taken over Rollins and Rollins when his father retired. The lawyer was probably a few years older and quite a bit grayer than Michelle, but there was a lot to be said—all of it good— about a man his age who still maintained a set of broad shoulders and a trim physique. "What do you think about him?" she asked.

"Who? Dave?" Michelle slid toward the end of the bench.

"Yes, Dave. We weren't discussing anyone else, were we?" Her friend's innocence didn't fool Erin. She'd seen the spark of interest in Dave's eyes, and she'd bet her bottom dollar Michelle had noticed, too.

"He's okay, I guess," Michelle hedged.

"Just 'okay'?" Erin framed the word in air quotes. Dave wasn't her type, but she could definitely see why her friend might find him attractive.

Michelle stilled. "I'm not looking for a new relationship," she argued. "It's only been a year since Allen…"

"I know. And I'm not suggesting you crawl in bed with the guy." She paused to take in the rosy flush that rose on Michelle's cheeks. "But there's no harm in being friends, is there?"

"Well, no. I suppose that'd be okay." Michelle pinned her with the kind of look that used to keep Ashley and Aaron from straying too far out of the lines. "Just don't get any crazy ideas. I have enough on my plate. I'm not going down that road."

*Whatever you say.*

"Gotcha," Erin said, letting her friend off that hook…for now.

As soon as Michelle headed upstairs to dress for the day, Erin picked up both mugs. She took them to the sink, where she poured the contents down the drain. Life was too short to pretend to enjoy cold coffee when a piping hot cup was only seconds away.

Carrying a fresh cup back to the table, she pulled up the Notes app on her cell phone and started making a short list of the things she wanted from the store. According to another app, the Sugar Sand Beach Grocery was only two miles down the road. She and Reggie could make a quick trip into Destin to drop off the rented trailers. When they returned, she'd promised to help Nina with the kitchen and check out the kayaks in the garage. But sometime today she'd head to the grocery store to stock up on basic necessities—like creamer and sugar for her best friend.

Wood smoke and the smell of ripened fruit laced the blast of cold air that struck Erin as the door to the Sugar Sand Beach Grocery swung shut behind her. "Good morning." She nodded to the portly gentleman who stood behind the lone cash register.

"Morning. How're y'all doing this fine morning?" His plump cheeks widening into a welcoming smile, he continued restocking the cigarette case over the counter. "Let me know if I can help you find anything."

"Thanks. I just might do that." Erin chose one of the three rickety carts parked near the entrance. The Sugar Sand Beach Grocery was definitely a throwback to another time, another era, she thought as, one of the cart's front casters wobbling madly, she headed down the first of a half dozen aisles. Cases of bottled water, as well as the most popular brands of sodas, had been stacked chest-high against the wall. Across from those, all manner of snack foods filled narrow shelves. Packages of hot dogs, lunch meats and sliced cheeses sat in an open cooler at the end of the row. She grabbed a wedge of cheddar and wrestled the stubborn cart around the corner and up what must be the bakery aisle. Here the options were more limited. Faced with the choice of white or wheat bread, she put a loaf of each in her cart. She threw in a package of hamburger buns for good measure. Individually wrapped cinnamon buns, six-packs of miniature donuts and boxes of something called Moon Pies crowded the end of the row. Cellophane snapped and popped as, more curious than hungry, she slipped one of the chocolate-covered desserts into her basket.

"I don't think I've seen you here before," the man behind the register called out when she reached the end of the aisle. "You visitin' or just passin' through?"

Erin leaned forward, her elbows braced on the cart's handle. Keeping the details to a minimum for now, she said, "A friend of mine owns property not far from here. I came down with her and a couple of our friends to help her fix up the place."

"She gonna sell it? 'Cause my sister-in-law's a Realtor. I can put you in touch."

Erin gave the man her best, friendliest smile. "Sugar Sand Beach is such a pretty little town, she's decided to make this her permanent home. I think we all might. But I'll remember to ask about your sister-in-law if she ever changes her mind." She let her gaze travel the collection of antiques that had been mounted on small shelves above the aisles. "I like the homey feel of your store. Have you been here long?"

"All my life. I took over the grocery when my dad retired. I'm Gus. That's my grandson, Little Gus, at the deli in the back. This'll all be his one day," Gus said, gesturing. Finished with the cigarettes, he picked up the empty box on the counter and carried it toward the back of the store.

Certain the owner would have more to say the next time she came within speaking range, Erin headed down the next aisle.

On either side of her, shallow shelves offered a narrow selection of canned and boxed goods. She checked the list Nina had pressed into her hand when she learned Erin was going shopping. The store stocked two types of flour—all-purpose and self-rising—but not the stone-ground, organic wheat the chef had requested. Erin grabbed the smallest bag of all-purpose and placed it in her cart. It would have to do until they made a trip to one of the larger stores in Destin. She added a sack of sugar before moving to the standalone cooler that served as the dairy section. Two pints of half-and-half and a carton of whole milk went into her cart. She searched through the rest of the shelves but, like the fancy flours and exotic oils on Nina's list, the store didn't carry almond milk.

The place wasn't all that large, and before long, she waited at the rear of the store where a towering "Little Gus" wore a haphazardly placed hairnet. From the scattering of pimples on his cheeks, she put his age somewhere in his twenties, but despite his youth, he handled the old-fashioned meat cutter well, making one paper-thin slice of ham after another. As he wrapped her order in thick, white butcher paper instead of tucking it into one of the plastic baggies favored by the larger grocery chains, the young man drawled, "You want smoked sausage? It's kind of our spe-ci-ality." He canted his head to the side. "We smoke it ourselves in the shack out back."

The smell of wood smoke that permeated the store making more sense, Erin asked, "It's good?"

"People come from all over for it." Little Gus's cheeks turned a lovely shade of scarlet. "We cook some up at lunchtime every day. The line sometimes stretches all the way to the door."

A ringing endorsement if she'd ever heard one. "I'll take a couple of pounds," she decided. She watched as the young man chose a yard-long strand of sausage from a white, enameled pan in the deli case. In a blur of motion, he slapped the sausage on the scale, cut off a three-pound piece, and wrapped it in butcher paper.

"Two pounds," he scrawled across the top using a thick, black crayon. "Enjoy," he said, smiling as he handed the package over the counter to her. "There's some mighty fine pickle relish on that shelf. One of the ladies in town makes it special just for us. Goes real good with the sausage. And hot dog buns, in case you forgot to get 'em."

"Thanks. I'll give it a try." Erin hefted her package. Crossing to a tall bookcase that served as the aisle's end cap, she added a pint-size Mason jar of relish and an eight-pack of buns to her cart. She smiled to herself. Little Gus might be young, but he'd mastered the art of upselling.

Tucked into one corner of the store, baskets of ripe, red tomatoes and apples sat on upended empty crates. Sandwiched between them, three wide, wooden trays held heads of iceberg lettuce, round, golden onions and bananas with speckled skins. Referring to Nina's list, Erin added a selection of fruits and vegetables to her cart.

She was nearly finished when the bell over the door at the front of the store tinkled. Seconds later, a boisterous man wearing a business suit struck up a conversation with Gus who, having finished stowing away the empty cigarette carton, had returned to his spot at the counter when Erin wasn't looking. She tried not to listen in, but that proved impossible considering she stood not a dozen steps from the register.

"Have you considered my offer yet, Gus?" The newcomer's voice practically echoed from the rafters.

Erin wasn't close enough to hear Gus's quieter response, but she assumed from the stranger's "C'mon, now, time's a-wasting" that whatever the man was offering, the store owner didn't want any part of it.

"Listen, Gus. There won't be much use for this place once Egret Bay opens. What with the influx of new residents and all, why, one of them big chain grocery stores'll be setting up shop here in Sugar Sand before you know it. You know good as I do, you can't compete with their lower prices. Next thing you know, they'll put you right out of business, and this is place won't be worth two cents. You need to act now." The newcomer brushed a hank of jet-black hair off his forehead.

Erin had lingered over the selection of personal products that filled the last aisle as long as she could. She pushed her cart a little closer to the register, stopping just shy of the end of the row.

The warmth apparent on Gus's face when she entered the store had disappeared. In its place, the store owner wore a guarded look as he swiped the counter with a rag. "I need more time to think about it, Orson," the older gentleman said, his tone not unkindly. "I'm not planning on throwing in the towel just yet.

This store's my grandson's future. I got to think about him."

"You just made my point," the man Gus had addressed as Orson said earnestly. "You gotta think about Little Gus back there." Gold glinted at his neck when he aimed a finger toward the deli section. As he did so, his gaze landed on Erin, where it lingered for several long heartbeats.

The predatory gleam that filled Orson's eyes made Erin feel like she wanted a long, hot shower with plenty of soap. She was relieved when, after giving her an appraising look, his focus shifted to the man behind the counter.

Orson cleared his throat. "You can't tell me this is all you want for your grandson—spending his days stocking shelves and mopping up spills. With the money you make from this deal, you can give him a life he'll be proud of."

Erin wasn't the least bit surprised when Gus stiffened. Insulting a potential customer headed her list of tips on how *not* to win friends and influence people.

Gus's voice dropped into a lower register. "I'm proud of what my dad built here." The man slapped his palm against the counter.

Erin had heard enough. The bully needed to have the wind taken out of his sails, and she knew just the way to do it. She pushed her cart all the way to the front of the store. "Orson, is it? Orson Danner?" Plastering an innocent look on her face, she extended a hand. "I'm Erin Bradshaw. Formerly of Fairfax, Virginia. Soon to be a resident of Sugar Sand Beach." She smiled sweetly. "My friends and I recently moved into the Simmons house."

The impact of that last sentence triggered the exact reaction she'd been hoping for. The interest that had flared in Orson's eyes faded faster than the green flash of a Key West sunset. The man's features hardened. He crossed his arms across a beefy chest.

"I heard a rumor that someone claiming to be related to Nancy Simmons had shown up. That's you?" Orson gave her a scornful look.

Erin was sorry her frayed shorts and well-worn T-shirt didn't measure up to Orson's standards, but she'd dressed to spend the day cleaning cupboards and sweeping out cobwebs, not impressing the local businessmen. "*My friend* is Ms. Simmons's sole heir," she corrected. "As a matter of fact, she's meeting with her attorney right now, signing the papers to legally transfer the property into her name."

Orson's face went blank as a freshly cleaned chalkboard. "Well, then. She's the person I'll need to talk to. I'll take that place off her hands. In this day and age, no one hangs on to a monstrosity like that old house."

"I wouldn't be too sure about that, Orson." Erin gave him another saccharine-sweet smile. "We think it's the perfect location for the inn we plan to open this fall."

"An inn?" Though Orson chortled as if she'd told a funny joke, his laughter carried a hollow note. "We'll see about that. The people who live around here won't tolerate a bunch of Northerners coming down here and ruining the place."

"But isn't that exactly what you and your associates were planning? That development you want to build...What'd you call it? Egret-Something? It would flood Sugar Sand Beach with an influx of part-time residents. It would put local shops like this one"—she glanced at Gus who stood, his cleaning rag in hand, watching intently—"out of business. You'd ruin the area with more traffic, more noise, more pollution."

"We prefer to think of Egret Bay as the opportunity for more jobs, more money flowing into the local—"

Erin cut him off. "All that money will flow one way—into the coffers of you and your business partners."

Orson's features hardened. His eyes narrowed into chips of blue ice. "I can see I'm wasting my time here. This is a matter for the town council to decide. Good luck with that," he said, sarcasm dripping from his voice. "They won't re-zone the property for some harebrained idea like opening an inn." Dismissive, he gave Gus a stern look. "I'll be back," he said, making the words sound more like a threat than a promise. "Be ready to accept my offer. You're running out of time."

Erin waited until the door slammed shut in Orson's wake before she took a deep breath. "Well, that was unpleasant," she muttered as the developer's Mercedes sped out of the parking lot. She turned to Gus. "I'm sorry if our little set-to upset you or your customers."

"What customers?" Gus waved a hand at the nearly empty store. He wrung the dry rag out and stuck it beneath the counter. "The man isn't wrong, you know. Sooner or later, things have to change. Maybe I'm a fool for resisting."

"I won't pretend to tell you how to run your business, Gus. But I will say this—your grandson back there is a natural-born salesman. Which I suspect is a trait he inherited from his grand-father. Just look at all the stuff he encouraged me to buy." Lifting the package of sausage, she pointed to the bottles of pickles and relish in her basket. "As for me and my friends," she said, starting to unload her purchases onto the counter, "we want Sugar Sand Beach to stay just as it is. We think our inn will help protect the things that make this area so special."

# Four

## Nina

Nina dipped her cleaning rag into the bucket of disinfectant and swiped it across the pantry shelf. She checked the cloth, satisfied when not a trace of dust or dirt appeared. Which was as it should be. After all, hadn't she spent the past two hours wiping down the shelves and prepping them for this final step?

Thinking of the hundreds of hours it would take to get the rest of the kitchen in shape, she hummed a happy tune. Yes, she had a lot of work ahead of her, but the prospect of running her very own kitchen made the effort worthwhile. She dunked her cleaning cloth in the bucket again, wrung it out, and methodically wiped down another section of the shelf. She hoped to finish with the pantry by the time Erin returned home with their first load of groceries.

*Home.*

Now that was a novel concept. Not one she'd ever applied to her last studio apartment, either. She'd lived most of her adult life in a series of tiny, one-room flats, borrowing a friend's strong back and truck long enough to move her few pieces of furniture to a different, cheaper place whenever her lease ran out or the landlord raised the rent. It hadn't really mattered where she lived, as long as it was within walking distance of the restaurant where she worked. That's where she spent most of her time—usually ten or twelve hours a day, six days a week. Granted, her work schedule didn't allow for much of a personal life, but she was okay with the occasional night out with her friends. When she stayed in, she had Mr. Pibbs to keep her company. But she'd known going in that rising to the top in her field, having her own kitchen one day, was going to take hard work and dedication. And yeah, she'd admit it—she'd totally blown her first chance at making a name for herself when she'd trusted the wrong man. That one move had cost her dearly, and it was probably a good thing she hadn't known how many years would fly by before a second chance came her way. If she had, maybe she'd have thrown in the towel back then. Or at least, stopped socking every spare dime away for the day when she'd see her own name above the door.

But now, at long last, she'd been handed the golden ticket—not just the chance to run a kitchen of her very own, but a permanent home with the three people she cared the most about in the entire world. If it took every penny she'd ever saved, if her back ached after a long day of scrubbing and cleaning and prepping, she'd deal with it. She'd do whatever it took to make the inn—and the café—a success. Her thoughts drifting to a future filled with the companionship of good friends, great food and happy customers, she finished the shelf she'd been working on and moved on to the next.

She'd finished one entire section and was about to replenish the disinfectant with a fresh batch when a door slammed. The sound of footsteps followed. She frowned. Had Erin returned sooner than expected? She studied the shelves she'd yet to wash and hoped not.

Seconds later, wearing frayed shorts and a grease-stained shirt, Reggie poked her head into the pantry. "Oh, hey. I thought Erin was helping you today. She's not here?"

"We needed a few things—bread, sandwich meat, coffee supplies. She went to the store." Nina picked up the bucket.

"Do you know how long she'll be gone? I was, um, sort of hoping to talk."

Reggie's dejected tone triggered Nina's inner alarm bells. She halted on her way to the deep sink to give the younger woman a closer look. Her shoulders slumped, her expression guarded, Reggie leaned against the door Nina had propped open. She'd shoved most of her strawberry-blond hair into a shapeless baseball cap, but a few strands had escaped. The girl either hadn't noticed or didn't care that the loose strands wore the same black grease that stained her shirt.

"Michelle's at the attorney's office. She planned to get the utilities transferred into her name while she was out and said not to expect her until sometime late this afternoon. Erin's getting the groceries. I gave her a pretty long list. She might be a while." Nina eyed Reggie's blotchy, tear-streaked face. Something was up, and since she didn't see any signs of an injury, she'd wager the trouble had something to do with Reggie's soon-to-be-ex. "I was just getting ready to take a break," she said, deciding to do so in that very instant. She set down the bucket and stepped out of the closet, which was large enough to hold a year's supplies. "You look like you need one, too. Join me."

"I hate to make you stop working. I know you're busy. But I need to talk to someone or I'm going to explode." Reggie's face filled with equal amounts of anger and confusion.

"What's up?" Nina hoisted herself up onto the granite surface of a kitchen counter. Someone had thoughtfully left a case of water at one end. She snagged a bottle and twisted the cap.

"It's Sam. He—oh, I don't know." Reggie pressed one hand over her eyes. She took a thready breath. "You don't need to listen to me and my problems. It feels like all I do these days is complain."

"You're entitled." The plastic made snapping noises as Nina rolled the water bottle back and forth between her fingers. "You don't see us giving Michelle a hard time every time she sheds a tear over Allen, do you?"

"No." Reggie exhaled forcefully. "But Sam didn't die. Much as sometimes I wish he had." Her eyes widening, she clamped a hand over her mouth. "I didn't mean that," she protested. "Honest, I didn't."

"It's okay," Nina encouraged. "We all say things we don't mean. No one here is going to hold it against you." She took a slug of water. "But your marriage did die," she said, not pulling any punches while she replaced the cap on the bottle. "The relationship with the one person you thought you'd spend the rest of your life with—it's over. I think that entitles you to complain or cry as much as you need to. You can even wish a plague of boils on Sam if that helps you feel better." Enough years had passed since her last bad breakup that she could sometimes think of the man who'd betrayed her without mentally reaching for a cast-iron frying pan, but the pain lingered. She'd battled the same hurt, anger and helplessness Reggie was feeling now.

"A swarm of hornets—that's what he deserves," Reggie declared.

"How about a sprinkle of ghost pepper in his morning cereal?" Nina asked, reviving one of her favorite revenge fantasies.

"Poison ivy in his tighty-whities."

"Ouch! That hurts." Nina grinned. "So, what's the pond scum done now?"

"Well." Reggie scuffed one sneakered foot against the floor. "It wasn't him so much as it was my divorce attorney. Last week he asked me to hold off on signing the separation agreement so he could dig a little deeper into our financials."

Nina nodded. Reggie had mentioned that

earlier. At the time, Nina thought the move sounded like a good plan. Though she'd never been married, there'd been a time or two when she wished she'd had someone looking out for her best interests like Reggie's lawyer was doing. From what Reggie had told them, Sam had already tried to dupe her into assuming responsibility for any bills they owed. If he'd do that, who knew what other tricks the man had up his sleeve? "Judging from how upset you were when you walked in here, I'm guessing the lawyer found something?"

"Another bank account. One Sam hadn't listed among our assets. The attorney was quite put out with me about it." Reggie held up her hands. "I didn't know anything about it, I swear. But it took a while to convince him I was completely in the dark."

"But he believes you now?" He'd better, or they'd all be thumbing through the Divorce Attorney section of the Yellow Pages.

"Yeah, he believes me. Now he just thinks I'm an idiot for not having a better idea of how much money my husband makes or that he's been socking so much of it away in an account I don't have access to." Reggie's head hung so low, her chin practically rested on her chest.

Taking in the other woman's rounded

shoulders and how she avoided making eye contact, Nina offered reassurance. "I'm sure there are plenty of women who don't know as much about their household finances as perhaps they ought to. The thing is, you'll never make that mistake again."

"I feel like such a fool." Reggie clambered up onto the counter beside Nina. "I believed Sam when he complained about how much money we owed or how tiny our apartment was. He always made such a big deal out of it when one of his friends moved into a big house. To hear him tell it, they all had nannies for their kids and sent them to private schools. He said we'd never be able to afford that kind of life, and he made me feel like it was my fault 'cause I didn't have a big, powerful job like his friends' wives did. He raised such a fuss if I spent too much money at the grocery store that sometimes I skipped lunch to make up for it. But while we were living on this shoestring budget, he was building a huge nest egg. Mr. Cole—he's my lawyer—he says Sam has over a hundred grand in that account. Meanwhile, we were living hand to mouth. Why would he do that?"

*Because Sam has something on the side.*

Everybody suspected that was the real reason Sam had walked away from his marriage.

Everybody but Reggie, that was. Her eyes were slowly opening to some of her ex's faults, but that was one conclusion she hadn't drawn…yet. For now though, Nina didn't feel like it was her job to point it out. For now, it was time to administer another dose of tough love.

"I can't tell you why Sam did what he did. But he's broken your trust. He's lied. He's gone behind your back. Just as bad—or maybe worse—he blamed you for problems that weren't your fault. I've known men like that. Heck, I was involved with a man like that. It nearly destroyed me."

"You?" Reggie's eyes filled with disbelief. "You'd never know it by looking at you. You're one of the most together people I know. You don't take guff from anybody."

"Is that your polite way of saying I'm a world-class shrew?" Nina deadpanned.

"Good grief—no!" Reggie recoiled in horror. "I didn't mean anything like that. I—"

"Relax." She jabbed her friend with an elbow. "I know what you meant. The restaurant business, like the landscaping business, is a male-dominated profession. I've had to learn to stand up for myself. The key word there was *learn*, in case you missed it. We all make mistakes. Yours was probably trusting Sam too much. Mine was, well, that's a story I don't tell unless there's wine involved. Lots of wine." She mimed pouring from two bottles at once. Dropping her hands to her lap, she shifted to face Reggie and added, "If we're lucky, we learn from our mistakes and move on. That's what you'll do. We're all here to help you do just that."

"I'm so glad I have you to lean on." Reggie's posture straightened. Bouncing a little as her feet touched the floor, she slid from the counter. "Seriously, Nina. I don't know what I would have done today if you hadn't been here."

"Aw, shucks, Reggie. T'weren't nothin'," Nina said in her best imitation of a Southern drawl. Her bottle of water was nearly empty. She downed the rest, brushed off her hands and stood. She studied her younger friend. The despair that had clung to Reggie like plastic wrap on the sides of a bowl had vanished. "You going to be okay?"

"I think I will be," Reggie said with renewed determination. "But if you and the others see me start to wilt, knock some sense into me, okay?"

"Count on it." Her fingers curled into a fist, Nina jabbed the air. She watched as, her head held high, Reggie headed out the door.

When she was gone, Nina shuddered a deep breath. The heart-to-heart had stirred up painful memories of a time when she'd been hopelessly, blindly in love with the wrong man. She'd been so convinced that she and Tobias were a team. And why wouldn't she when he talked of the day the two of them would open their own place and set the restaurant world on fire. She'd been so convinced of their future together that she'd created innovative recipes for him and made excuses when he lost his temper or flirted with the other cooks on the line. When he'd railed that her dishes weren't up to his exacting standards, she'd told herself that all chefs were tempera-mental. The demand for perfection was what made the great ones great, and, like a fool, she'd tried harder. She'd refused to believe that by adding a touch more salt or a few grains of pepper, Tobias was making her dishes his. Or that, when opportunity did come knocking, he'd walk through the door without her. But the real betrayal came when she'd dared to protest. That's when he'd pointed an accusing finger at her, told everyone who'd listen she was trying to steal recipes that were his alone, and left her behind with her reputation in tatters, her heart broken.

Fixing her heart had been easy enough. Once the tears had slowed and the blinders had come off, she'd sworn she'd never let herself be that vulnerable again. So far, she hadn't. She doubted she ever would.

Her career, though, had been far more difficult to rebuild. Tobias's lies had spread from kitchen to kitchen with all the contagion of a plague. Accused of trying to steal recipes from the hottest new chef on the restaurant scene, she'd been blackballed, relegated to the lowest-paying jobs in the industry. Only in the last five years had she been able to once again climb the ladder from prep cook to head saucier. But then Chad had come along. The stiffness in her shoulders loosened. The sous chef hadn't meant to do her any favors, but if he hadn't messed with her work, she might have been content— not exactly thrilled perhaps, but content—to stay in that position for the rest of her career.

But now thanks to Michelle, Erin and Reggie—and yes, Chad—she had a second chance to fulfill a lifelong dream. Aware of how seldom such an opportunity came along, she determined to do everything in her power to see that the café at Sugar Sand Inn became a huge success. She grabbed the bucket of disinfectant and toted it to the deep sink. After replacing the cleanser with a fresh batch, she returned to the pantry and began scrubbing the rest of the shelves in earnest.

# Five

## Reggie

Five hours later, after tending to the special secret project Reggie had hidden behind the gardener's shed, she disconnected the battery cables from the tractor she and Erin had discovered on their first visit to the house Michelle had inherited. Reggie climbed onto the seat of the John Deere and, for the second time today, twisted the key in the ignition. The engine sputtered but just as quickly died. She crossed her fingers, counted to ten and tried again. This time, a throaty roar echoed off the unfinished concrete walls. Grinning, she fist-pumped the warm, humid air. The third time was, indeed, the charm.

She'd say one thing for the person who'd taken care of Nancy Simmons's property these last five years—they sure knew their engines. As soon as she met their intrepid handyman, she'd give him a huge thank-you. Anxious to start clearing the overgrowth around the property, she'd spent the morning checking belts, lubing all the moving parts, adding oil, and refilling all the tractor's fluid levels. She hadn't had much hope that after sitting so long, the old workhorse would start right up, though. To her surprise, it had required only a minimal amount of tinkering to get the motor humming.

She'd driven a later model of the same beast when she worked for a landscape business in Virginia. Familiar with the controls, she shifted the tractor into gear and slowly backed it out of the shed. She eased onto the concrete pad in front of the garage, where she let the engine idle for a bit. The last thing she wanted was to get halfway across the five acres surrounding the house and have Ol' Betsy, here, conk out on her.

Five minutes later, the oil pressure remained steady. When the motor continued to purr like a kitten with a bad sinus infection, she once more put the tractor in gear. She'd barely moved ten feet when the back door of the house opened. Nina waved from the top step with one hand while making a slicing motion across her throat with the other.

"What's up?" she shouted over the noisy engine.

Instead of answering, Nina only repeated the side-to-side gesture across her neck.

"Okay, okay." Reggie shot Nina a good-natured smile. In answer to the request, she powered down the tractor.

"Can you take a break?" Nina called once the rustle of a balmy breeze through the trees was the only sound. "Michelle and Erin are back. They've called a house meeting."

Reggie frowned. Michelle was supposed to meet with Dave Rollins this morning to finalize the move of the Simmons property into her name. Had something gone wrong? Hating the thought of what it might mean for the Sugar Sand Inn if the transfer hadn't gone as planned, Reggie hustled down from the tractor.

"Any idea what this is all about?" she asked when she reached the steps that led up to the sun porch at the rear of the house.

"No. Just that Michelle said we all needed to talk. They're in the family room."

"Where is that again?" The rambling, two-story house had more twists and turns than a corn maze. Maybe after a week or so, she'd learn her way around, but she'd gotten lost on her way to the stairs this morning.

"Straight through the kitchen. Down the hall to the left. Just past the formal dining room." Nina laughed. "I think we're going to need a map."

"That would come in handy," Reggie said as she toed off her work boots so she wouldn't track more dirt through the house than absolutely necessary. Speaking of which…She glanced down at her shirt and shorts. Working on the tractor had stained her clothes with grease and oil. She had a feeling Michelle wouldn't appreciate it if any of it rubbed off on the furniture. "Give me five minutes to run upstairs and wash up."

"Okay, but…"

Reggie felt Nina's searching gaze on her. "What?"

"I haven't told anyone about our talk this morning. I figured that was your business."

Reggie swept her hat from her head. The reddish curls she'd stuffed inside the cap sprang free and tumbled halfway down her back. "You're welcome to bring them up to speed while I dash upstairs to change. I'm not trying to keep my problems with Sam a secret." There were other things she hadn't shared with her friends, but her troubles with Sam weren't among them.

She headed for the back staircase, where she took the steps to the second floor two at a time.

It took a little longer than she'd anticipated to scrub the grease from under her fingernails, but she was only a few minutes late when she walked into the den wearing a fresh pair of shorts and a clean T-shirt. Curtains billowed in the cool breeze that blew in through the open windows. Someone had taken the time to whisk the sheets off the furniture. Sofas, love seats and side chairs had been arranged in attractive groupings about the spacious room. Michelle, Erin and Nina had spread out on two tan leather couches in front of a fireplace. The beverages of their choice rested on the wide coffee table in front of them.

"Brought this for you." Nina held out a bottle of water.

"Thanks." Reggie accepted the drink, though, judging from the three sober faces in the room, she wondered if the occasion might call for something stronger. Apprehension stirred in her belly. She sank onto the couch and held her breath. If things hadn't gone well at the attorney's office, the others might pack up and head back to Virginia. But where would that leave her? She'd given up the apartment she and Sam had shared. Not only that, but in preparation for moving into Michelle's fully-furnished house, she'd sold or given away all but a few pieces of furniture and essentials. Her mouth dry, she took a drink of water. Might as well get right to the point, she decided and asked, "How'd things go with Dave Rollins?"

All eyes turned to Michelle, who cleared her throat. "Smooth as silk. I am now officially the proud owner of all this." A wave of her hand indicated the house and beyond. "The question is, can I—can we—hang on to it?"

"I thought we already crossed that bridge. We satisfied the tax lien." Erin and Nina had pitched in to pay the overdue tax bill. "You wouldn't do that just to sell the place, would you? Aren't the rest of us going to help you turn this into the Sugar Sand Inn?" Feeling like she'd been sent out onto the field without ever reading the playbook, Reggie studied the faces of her friends. Michelle's and Erin's bore nearly identical concerned expressions. Nina, though, looked as baffled as she felt.

The chef stretched out her long, lean legs and propped her bare feet on one corner of the coffee table. "We are moving forward with those plans, aren't we?"

"Yes."

Michelle's firm assurance should have quieted the butterflies in Reggie's stomach, but they still beat frantic wings.

"There is a problem, though," Michelle conceded. She glanced at the woman seated at the opposite end of the couch. "Erin ran into Oscar Danner at the grocery store this morning. He, um— To say he's not happy about our plan to convert this place into an inn would be an understatement."

"I think his exact words were—" Erin leaned forward. Her voice rose several decibels. "'We won't tolerate a bunch of Northerners coming down here and ruining the place.' He said he'd put a stop to what he called 'this nonsense' at the next town council meeting."

"Sounds like a heated conversation." Nina uncrossed and recrossed her ankles. "How'd you two happen to meet?"

"Orson was pressuring Gus—he's the owner of the Sugar Sand Beach Grocery—to sell out. And Gus, well, he's a sweetie. Older gentleman. He's owned the grocery store for forty years, plans on keeping it in the family. Orson clearly wasn't taking 'no' for an answer, and things were getting uncomfortable. I mean, Orson's loud— you could hear him all over the store. I didn't intend to get into anything with him. Just walked up and introduced myself. Told him we'd moved into the Simmons place, and that was all it took. He went off like Mount Fuego."

Reggie's fingers tightened around her water bottle. Her sister had been in Guatemala when the volcano erupted and had helped out with the relief efforts.

"Can he shut us down?" she asked. Granted, she didn't have the financial stake in the inn like her other three friends, but she'd invested just as much of her hopes and dreams in making it a success. "He's just one man with one opinion, isn't he?"

"I don't know, to be honest," Erin said, her expression glum. "After Orson stormed out—he literally burned rubber when he pulled out of the parking lot—Gus and I chatted while he rang up my groceries." She scanned the room. "By the way, calling it a grocery store is a bit of a stretch. It's more like an oversize convenience store. I couldn't get quite a few things on your list, Nina. But they did have some sausage that smells incredible."

"We'll make do." The chef shrugged. "Right now, I'm more interested in what Gus had to say."

Erin nodded. "He seemed to think Orson could make serious trouble for us. Evidently, the man has a lot of clout in the area. We thought our zoning request would sail through the town council. After all, they were going to approve

Orson's proposal for a hundred homes. It seemed like a no-brainer that they'd approve our plan to re-zone it commercial as long as we maintained the property as it is. But if Orson gets the neighbors and townsfolk on his side, the council might turn down our zoning request. Without that, we won't be able to get a business license."

"We're not going to let him win, though, are we? I mean, we are going to fight, right?" First Sam, now this Orson fellow. The whole idea of men who had awfully high opinions of themselves pushing her around was getting old, thought Reggie.

"Of course we'll fight." A leather cushion creaked as Michelle stood. She strode to the fireplace and turned to face them. "We are not going to walk away from our dream just because Orson ruffled his feathers," she said firmly. Her voice softening, she added, "The problem is, I'm not sure of the best way to get everyone else to see our side of things."

"Maybe we need to get out and mingle with the community. Let everyone know who we are and that we're here to stay," Nina suggested.

"That'd be a good start," said Erin. "But I think we need to do more. Gus was really nice at the grocery store today. Friendly. Warm. He definitely is not a big fan of Orson's. But…" Her voice trailed off.

"But he's not willing to buck the tide for complete strangers, right?" Reggie finished.

"Right," Erin nodded. "Especially if it means he'll end up selling to Orson eventually but for less money."

"If we fail, you mean." Reggie bit her bottom lip while she assessed the matter before them like she would a complicated landscape design. "It sounds like we need a two-pronged approach," she suggested. "First, we have to help everyone see that selling out to Orson would be a bad idea."

"That's the easy part," Erin said. "Only someone who's had their head buried in the sand would think Orson's plan is a good thing." According to Dave Rollins, Orson and a cadre of investors had hoped to snap up the land Michelle had inherited from her birth mother. But razing the Simmons house and developing the five acres around it had only been the first step in the businessman's plan to build a new residential community. He and his financial backers were offering top dollar for businesses like Gus's, in the hopes of transforming the sleepy beachside community into a bustling resort town. "If he moves forward, five years from now, there won't be anything left of Sugar Sand Beach."

Reggie was sure Erin hadn't meant to criticize her idea, but her sister's remark told her that her approach was far too simple for the complicated problem they faced. She let out a long, slow breath and tucked herself farther into her corner of the couch. She'd be better off letting the older, wiser heads take the lead on this one.

"You said there were two parts," prodded Nina when Reggie didn't say anything more. "What's the rest?"

"Oh, that's okay." Reggie shook her head. "It's probably a dumb idea anyway." At least, that's what Sam usually called her suggestions.

"There are no dumb answers," Michelle corrected. "We're brainstorming solutions here, and we want to hear yours."

"Okay, but..." Reggie took a calming breath and straightened when even Erin looked at her expectantly. "Well, I think next, we need to let everyone get to know us. We have to show them what we have in mind for the inn and why we're offering a better choice for Sugar Sand Beach."

"I like that," Michelle said encouragingly. "Any suggestions on how to go about it?"

Reggie plunged ahead. "I was thinking, what if we put together a kind of reverse welcome package? Something that says, 'We're new to the area, and we want to introduce ourselves.' Maybe add a little brochure about us and our ideas for the inn, the café."

"Oooh, I like that." Sitting forward, Nina lowered her feet to the floor. "I'm picturing gift baskets filled with goodies. All of it somehow tied to Sugar Sand Inn, of course. I'd be happy to bake enough cookies and other treats. Let's see—we'd want to use a Florida theme, so how about lemon bars and pecan sandies?"

"Mmmm. My mouth is watering already," Michelle said.

Erin raised her hand. "I'll make the brochure."

"You can count on my help, too," Reggie added. She wasn't much of a cook, but she'd had a summer job making gift baskets once. She could tie a mean bow.

"So we're all agreed? We're going to do this? We'd want to hand-deliver the baskets to every member of the town council, plus the owners of most of the businesses around here." When the others nodded, Michelle asked, "Do we know the names of the council members?"

"Not offhand," Erin answered. "But the information should be easy enough to find out. They're probably listed on the town's website. As for business owners, the Chamber of

Commerce will have a list. I'll look it up when we finish here."

Michelle's shoulders shifted. "I'm not sure that's enough, though. We want to make a solid impression if we're going to get everyone in Sugar Sand Beach on our side."

Reggie hesitated. So far, everyone had been receptive to her ideas, but this next one would take a lot more effort than putting together a few baskets. When no one jumped in with another suggestion, she took a breath. "What if we held an open house? Maybe the week before the next town council meeting? Or, if that's too soon, before the one where they vote on our request to change the zoning?" She'd never been to a town council meeting in her life and had no idea how they were run, but if it was like any committee she'd ever joined, things got put on the agenda one month and were voted on at the next meeting. She glanced around the room. Dust and five years' worth of grime covered every surface. They'd need as much lead time as they could get in order to make the downstairs ready for company.

"We can invite everyone for miles around, let them see what we're doing here, how we're contributing to the local economy without destroying the very things that make Sugar Sand Beach so special." Having said her piece, Reggie looked to Michelle for approval.

"What? Don't look at me," the dark-haired brunette protested. "We're all in this together."

"True," Reggie pointed out. "But as the owner, it's really up to you."

"Hmm." Michelle cupped her chin in one hand. "That brings up another topic. One that's just as important as what we've been discussing. I'd intended to talk about it tonight over dinner, but we're all here now, so…"

"What's on your mind?" Nina wanted to know.

"I told you things went very well at the attorney's this morning," Michelle paused, her gaze flitting from face to face.

Reggie nodded along with everyone else, though disappointment rippled through her at the unexpected change of topics. She'd wanted to nail down the details for the open house.

"How is our favorite lawyer?" Erin asked when Michelle's focus landed on her. "Still as handsome as he was the last time you saw him?"

Reggie couldn't help but grin when Michelle colored slightly.

"Oh, stop," the widow protested. "I told you. I'm not interested right now."

"But someday? Maybe?" Erin asked with a lighthearted jab.

"Sto-op," Michelle said firmly. "This is important."

"Okay, Mom. I'll be good." Erin sighed like she used to whenever their mom reminded her to take out the trash for the third time, but she grabbed her can of soda and sat back. "What is it?"

"I intend to ask Dave to look into what it would take to form a legal partnership between the four of us. As soon as he sets it up, I'll transfer ownership of this house, the land, all the other assets Nancy left me into this new entity."

Shock waves rippled through the room. As Erin grasped the significance of what Michelle was offering, her eyes grew so large, she looked like a hoot owl when she blinked. Nina's mouth dropped open, and a surprised gasp rang out. Long seconds passed before either of them could speak. Reggie watched as Erin recovered first. Her sister's feet hit the floor. She leaned over, her elbows balanced on her knees. "Are you serious?" she asked.

"Dead serious," came Michelle's answer.

"But why?" Nina asked.

Michelle's hands dropped to her sides. "A

couple of reasons. First, you're my best friends. We've been through a lot over the years, and we've always stuck by one another. I don't know what I'd do without you."

"We feel the same way," Nina said while Erin and Reggie nodded their agreement.

"Also, you deserve it. I realize each of us had reached a crossroads in recent months. Nina— that new sous chef was gunning for your job." She waited for the leggy brunette's nod before she pinned Reggie with a look. "Your life had just fallen apart." Turning to Erin, she said, "You were ready for a fundamental change." Michelle held out one hand, her palm up. "Still, none of you had to move here. You could have stayed put and toughed it out. Instead, you gave up your lives in Virginia, put your trust in me, in this dream we share. If we're going all in on this, you deserve as much say in what happens as I do. A partnership will give you that. Plus, it protects your interests in case I'm suddenly out of the picture."

"You're not planning on going anywhere, are you?" Reggie rushed to ask.

"No." The precisely cut edges of Michelle's hair shimmied. "But if this year has taught me anything, it's that we're not guaranteed a set amount of time on this earth. Besides…" She grinned. "You all know what a worrywart I am.

If I had to manage all this on my own, I'd probably end up in the hospital with ulcers."

"No!" Erin clapped a hand over her mouth, mirth glinting in her eyes. "You—obsessive?" She shook her head. "It's nice to hear you finally admit it."

"We all have our crosses to bear." Michelle shrugged and seemed mesmerized by the fringe on the thick Oriental carpet for a moment. When she looked up, her eyes pleaded with them. "So, please, you'd be doing me a favor by joining me in this partnership."

Erin sprang from the couch, crossed the room and embraced Michelle in a tight squeeze. "I'll put everything I have into making the Sugar Sand Inn a success," she swore.

Nina was next. She crowded in, wrapping her arms around both Michelle and Erin. "Thank you," the tall, willowy chef said. "I'll never be able to repay you for this opportunity, but I'll do my level best to help the inn and café exceed our wildest expectations."

Tears welled in Reggie's eyes. The gift was incredibly generous, and even though she'd have to turn it down, she joined the others in a group hug. "Thanks for the offer," she whispered in Michelle's ear while Nina and Erin pressed in on either side.

Despite a sour, sinking feeling in her stomach, Reggie put on a happy face and, for the next few minutes, pretended to join in while the others celebrated their good fortune. Once the celebration died down a bit, though, she reached for Michelle's hand and gave it a squeeze. "I'm so happy for the three of you. Really I am." She swiped at a rogue tear with her free hand. "But I'm afraid your new company will have to have three members, not four. I can't be a part of it."

A look of pure incredulousness swept over Michelle's face. "Why not?" she gasped. From close by, Nina and Erin registered the same shock.

Tears welled in Reggie's eyes. She squeezed them shut and willed herself not to cry. "Sam," she said, answering as succinctly as she could.

"What's your soon-to-be ex- have to do with any of this?" Michelle asked.

"I found out earlier today that he's been squirreling money away in a secret bank account. Quite a lot of money."

Michelle and Erin both sucked in quick breaths.

Reggie waved a hand. "Don't worry. My attorney's all over it like bees on clover. But Sam's not going to be very happy about giving up his nest egg. And if I know him—which I

LEIGH DUNCAN

think I do—if he ever found out I was part owner of a valuable piece of property in Florida, he'd want to get his greedy hands on it. We'd be forced to buy him out, or worse, let him be involved in every decision, every move we make. That's not something I'd wish on my worst enemy, much less my best friends."

"What about after the divorce is final?" Nina looked to Michelle. "Couldn't we hold a place for Reggie and add her later?"

Reggie scuffed her foot against the floorboards. As tempting the suggestion sounded, she didn't think it would work. "The way things are going, it could be a year or more before we sign the separation agreement. The divorce won't be final for another six months after that. But even then, if Sam ever found out…well, I don't know the legal ramifications, but you can bet your bottom dollar he does, and if there's a way to butt in, he'll find it. It—it's not worth the risk." Though her voice remained firm, tears dripped down her cheeks. She brushed them away.

"Much as I hate to agree with her, I think Reggie's right, Michelle," Erin said with a sigh. "Sam's already proven he can't be trusted. It'd be foolish to give him a chance to get a piece of what we're going to build."

Reggie gave her sister a weak smile. She was

100

pretty sure Erin thought she'd been a fool for getting involved with Sam in the first place.

Nina wiped a few stray tears from her eyes with a napkin she'd pulled from a pocket. "I think you ought to talk to Dave about this, Michelle. See if he can't find a legal work-around."

"Good idea. We'll see what he says." Michelle gave a brisk, businesslike nod. "But no matter what, as far as I'm concerned, from this moment forward, this is a four-way partnership." She surveyed the others. When they'd voiced their own agreement, she cleared her throat. "Which reminds me, there won't be a Sugar Sand Inn unless we can win over the townsfolk. So, what's this about an open house? I'd like to hear more about that."

Reggie blotted her cheeks and eyes. She might be a partner in name only, but it felt good to be part of the group. She named a few of the things they'd have to accomplish before inviting the public into the house. "We'll need to spruce up the front and thoroughly clean the down-stairs. Michelle can work her decorating magic in a few areas, and we should serve food—maybe cocktails and appetizers?"

Over the next half hour, they made an initial list of action items aimed at getting what Erin jokingly referred to as Operation Open House in motion. Then they headed off in different directions, each eager to get started on their assigned tasks. Or at least, Reggie thought they were heading in different directions until Erin caught up with her on the stairs.

"You okay?" her sister wanted to know. "It couldn't have been easy to hear that Sam has been holding out on you all this time."

"I won't lie. It kind of broke me inside," Reggie admitted. "We might not have had much, but I'd convinced myself that as long as we loved each other and were honest with each other, we'd be okay. Turns out I was lying to myself, just like Sam was lying to me...about everything."

"I'm so sorry, Reggie," Erin offered.

"I'll be all right," she said, accepting her sister's sympathy. The temptation to tell Erin the rest of it tugged at her, but she decided not to as they reached the top of the stairs and headed for their own rooms. For now, at least, she kept the worst part to herself. As close as she'd grown to Erin in the past few weeks, she wasn't sure her sister—or anyone else for that matter—could comprehend how badly Sam had betrayed her. Because the whole time they'd been scrimping and saving and going deeper and deeper into debt to pay for one fertility treatment after another, her husband had had enough money squirreled away to make their dream of having a baby—making a family—come true...and he'd never said a word about it. Which, more than anything else Sam had done, hurt the most.

# Six

## Michelle

*I* guess today's the day we find out if the roof leaks," Michelle announced to no one in particular. Her brows drawn bowstring-tight, she stared beyond the kitchen window at the rain that poured by the bucketful out of a darkened sky. A brisk wind sent sheets of rain skittering across the grass. Fat drops pelted the windows. Water ran in rivers from the gutters. Thunder boomed overhead. In the distance, lightning flashed.

"We sure picked the right day to work inside." A pale yellow ribbon in her hand, Reggie glanced up from the gift basket she'd just covered in clear cellophane. A week had passed since their meeting in the family room. Operation Open House was in full swing. In her role as gardener/landscaper, she'd spent most of her time clearing out the overgrowth at the entrance, trimming the hedges around the house and creating a test bed in the garden. "I hope my new plants don't get washed away."

"So do I. I'm looking forward to those fresh herbs," Nina said. She'd suggested that Reggie plant a few of her favorites.

Another bolt of lightning lit the sky. At nearly the same time, thunder cracked.

"We're cooking with gas, but I still wouldn't like it if we lost power," Nina continued. She slid a tray of unbaked cookies into the Aga's massive oven. Slipping off her oven mitts, she picked up a pastry bag filled with lemon-colored icing. She bent over an array of cookies in various beach-themed shapes. Each had been outlined in yellow. Choosing one, she positioned the icing tip a precise quarter of an inch away from the surface and began working the nozzle from side to side in close lines. In seconds, the lines blurred as the icing spread. By the time she finished with it, glossy yellow flooded the cookie's top. Nina lifted the nozzle and moved on to the next one. She completed three others before the timer on the stove dinged. Her movements fluid, she set the pastry bag aside, slipped her hand into the waiting oven mitt and removed the cookie sheet.

"Are there any more?"

"That's the last of them," the remaining woman in the kitchen answered. Erin pointed to the bowl that had been filled with cookie dough two hours earlier. While Nina had alternated between baking and decorating, she'd rolled and cut batch after batch. She gathered a few tiny scraps of dough and tossed them into the nearby trash can.

"Anyone know when this rain will let up?" Michelle asked. Abandoning her post at the window, she crossed the room to the table where she and Reggie had spent the morning assembling two dozen gift baskets for the movers and shakers of Sugar Sand Beach.

"It's supposed to last another hour before things start to calm down, according to the weather reports," Erin said as she carried the empty bowl to the sink. "Some kind of front is blowing through. Tomorrow, we'll be back to clear, sunny skies."

"With all this rain, I'm concerned about the driveway," Michelle said. "The washer and dryer are supposed to be delivered tomorrow." Much to everyone's dismay, the ten-year-old pair of appliances in the laundry room had deteriorated beyond repair. "What do you think, Reggie? Can the truck get here without getting stuck?"

"Depends. A pickup truck won't have any trouble. But if they send one of those big box trucks, you might want to put a pin in that." Reggie shook her head. "It'll be too muddy for them to make it all the way up from the street." She glanced up as a particularly strong gust of wind buffeted the house.

Michelle shivered despite the warmth of the kitchen. Her home in Fairfax had a basement where she could take shelter whenever a strong storm blew through. But the water table in Florida was too high for a basement...unless the owner planned on turning it into a below-ground swimming pool. She cast a wary eye out the window in time to see a palm frond sail by.

*Enough!*

She needed a distraction. Grabbing an empty basket, she crumpled bubble wrap into the bottom. This she covered with a layer of green filler. Erin had picked up a case of yellow water bottles for a dollar apiece from a store in Destin. One of those went in next, followed by a jar of local honey.

"There's so much other work to do, I was hoping to put it off for a bit. But with rain like this, I'd better move it up on the schedule. I'll get started on it tomorrow," Reggie said, still talking about the driveway.

"Won't a whole new driveway be horribly expensive?" Michelle pictured cement trucks lined up for miles.

"Um, we already have gravel," Reggie pointed out. "It's just been mashed down over the years and needs to be refreshed. I'll grade the driveway, use the box scraper to bring the gravel back up to the surface, then level it out. It'll take a day or two, but it'll look real nice when I'm finished."

Michelle had no idea what a box scraper was, but she caught the gist of the matter. "So just labor?"

"We might need another truckload of stone. I can't tell till I get in there with the scraper. If we do, we can save money by spreading it ourselves."

"With rakes?" Michelle stifled a groan. Just the thought of shoveling and raking the entire distance from the house to the road made her back complain. But Reggie was right—they couldn't ask their guests to risk getting stuck whenever it rained. Nor could she sell the idea of traipsing around in the mud as some kind of hippy-dippy spa treatment.

"Well, you could if you want to, but it'll go a lot faster and easier if we use the tractor." Reggie grinned.

"You had me going there for a second,"

Michelle admitted. She plucked one of the individually wrapped banana muffins from a tray on the table. While Erin and Nina laughed, she went through an exaggerated windup and pretended to pitch one straight at Reggie, who feigned a batter ducking out of the batter's box.

Instead of tossing the muffin, Michelle selected another one and arranged them in the basket between the water bottle and the honey. She picked up one of the colorful, tri-fold brochures Erin had created and neatly wedged it between the taller items. Propping cookies shaped like seashells and a tray of lemon bars in front, she stood back to judge her work. The cookies weren't quite right, she decided. She shifted one closer to the edge and smiled. Straightening, she worked on loosening muscles that had grown tight from spending the morning bent over the work table.

"I'll get started on the driveway tomorrow." Reggie centered the basket on a large sheet of cellophane. A bit of the green fiber had dribbled down the outside. She tucked in where it belonged. Plastic crackled sharply as she pulled the corners of the plastic sheeting up and over the taller items. After securing the ends with a pipe cleaner, she finished the whole thing off with a neat yellow bow. Standing back, she admired her handiwork. "People are going to love these," she declared. "Are you and Erin planning to deliver them tomorrow?"

Michelle shrugged. They'd agreed to drop a basket off with each of the seven members of the town council, as well as all of the area's business owners. "Depends on whether or not the Escalade can make it to the street."

"You can take my truck," Reggie offered. "It might not be as fancy, but it'll handle a little mud." Gently, she rolled the leftover cellophane into a tube, which she secured with a rubber band on either end.

"We might have to take you up on that. But for now"—Michelle pushed herself away from the table—"I could use a cup of coffee. What about everyone else?"

"I wouldn't mind some," Erin said. She headed for a cupboard where she took down four of the mugs she and Nina had washed and dried and stored away after treating the entire kitchen to a thorough scrubbing.

Finished flooding the cookies with icing, Nina chose six slightly imperfect ones. These she arranged on a small plate. "Do we have any of that French Roast left?"

"Sorry, I think we used the last of it this morning." Michelle frowned. In just over a week, the four of them had put a serious dent in her supply of K-Cups. "I've added it to the list for our next trip to the grocery store."

"Ummm. I wouldn't count on finding any at Gus's. That's more of a Destin item," Erin said. She slipped a pod of medium roast into the Keurig. Seconds later, the aroma of fresh-brewed coffee filled the air.

Meanwhile, Michelle had retrieved the creamer from the refrigerator. She took it, along with spoons and napkins, to the table in the breakfast nook where a sugar bowl and glass container of artificial sweetener sat. Reggie grabbed two of the mugs of coffee her sister had brewed. At the table, she slid one in front of Michelle, the other in front of Nina, who'd placed the plate of cookies beside a stack of napkins before sliding onto the bench seat. Carrying the other two cups, Erin joined them. She handed one to Reggie, and they both sat.

Outside, a bright white light pulsed.

Michelle flinched. "Yikes. That was close, wasn't it?"

Reggie counted, "One one-thousand. Two one-thousand. Three one-thousand…" She reached seven before thunder rumbled overhead. "About a mile away. But if it's any consolation, I think the worst of the storm is past us."

"I'll be glad when it's over," Michelle confessed. She hunched her shoulders around her ears like a turtle retreating from danger.

"Here." Erin held out the plate of cookies. "Take one. A little bit of sugar and some caffeine will perk you right up."

"I shouldn't. I had one earlier." Michelle hesitated. She'd been meaning to start her diet every day for the last month. Not that she needed to lose that much. Between sorting and packing her household goods in Virginia and all the effort she'd put into making the various rooms of the new place shine, the extra fifteen pounds she'd been so concerned about six weeks ago had simply melted away. Deciding one little cookie wouldn't hurt, she chose the smallest. The treat broke in half with a satisfying snap. Taking a bite, she nodded to Nina. "These are divine."

"You don't think they're overdone, do you?" Nina chose one shaped like a cone shell and turned it upside down. She examined the golden-brown underside. "Guess not," she said, answering her own question. "I'm still learning how the Aga works. It's a dream, but it has its quirks."

Reggie spoke around a mouthful of cookie. "Everyone is going to take one taste of these and vote in favor of the Sugar Sand Inn and Café."

She brushed a few crumbs into her cupped palm and wrapped them in a napkin.

"Speaking of which, what time did you want to get started tomorrow?" Erin directed the question to Michelle.

"Nine? Nine thirty?" Michelle took a sip of coffee.

"I'll go out early and take a look at the mud situation," Reggie offered. She pulled the scrunchie from her hair, fluffed the long curls loose and re-captured them in a haphazard ponytail. "You know, I'm surprised no one ever did anything about that driveway before."

"Everyone says Nancy was a bit of a recluse." Erin folded her napkin into a neat triangle. "She probably didn't want to encourage visitors."

"Where we want as many as we can get." Michelle tugged her bottom lip between her teeth. After reading Nancy Simmons's letter, she'd spent a considerable amount of time thinking about her birth mother's tragic life. The more she thought about Nancy's story, the more she wanted to heal the breach with her own children. Oh, sure, she could tell herself all day and all night she wasn't the one with the problem, that Ashley and Aaron had chosen to turn their backs on her, not the other way around. But when she got right down to it, as their mother, she was the responsible adult. It was up to her to make sure the twins knew they'd always be her first priority.

Taking another sip of coffee, she studied the faces of her friends. They'd all been so supportive, offering laughs or shoulders to lean on when Ashley didn't return her calls or Aaron's clipped responses made it clear he was still angry with her. But would they support her next idea?

*You'll never know if you don't ask.*

She took a breath and plunged in. "As long as we're all here together, I, um, I have a favor to ask."

"Whatcha need?" Interest glowed in Reggie's blue eyes.

"Yeah, what's up?" Without taking a bite, Nina slipped the cookie she'd been studying onto the plate.

Erin simply folded her hands and waited. She knew Michelle well enough to trust her to provide all the details in good time.

"I'd like to invite Aaron and Ashley down in two weeks...for Mother's Day weekend. Would everybody be okay with that?" She held her breath, knowing her relationship with her children hung in the balance.

"Are the three of you getting along better these days?" Nina pushed a wayward strand of hair from her face.

"Well, no. Not exactly." Much as she wanted to say everything was peachy-keen and having the twins down for a visit would be fun for everyone, Michelle wouldn't lie to her friends. Her voice thickened. "The truth is, Ashley still isn't returning my phone calls. Aaron and I have spoken a few times, but he's so cool and distant, it's like talking to a stranger."

"So why, exactly, do you think having them here is a good idea?" Erin asked over the rim of her coffee cup.

"I have to do *something*. I can't let things go on the way they are." She brushed her hair behind her ears. "I hope once they see this place and hear our plans for it, some of our enthusiasm for the inn will rub off on them. That they'll realize I didn't just pull up stakes in Virginia and move south without thinking it through."

Nina toyed with the spoon she'd used to stir her coffee. "You know the problem isn't that you've moved to Florida to open an inn, don't you? It's that you had to sell the home they grew up in."

"When our folks sold their place in Fairfax and moved to West Virginia, I struggled with it for a bit," Reggie admitted. She rubbed at a wet spot on the table with her balled up napkin. "I was grown and married and thought I had my life all figured out, but it still bothered me. For Ashley and Aaron, this move has to be even more difficult."

Erin stared at Reggie for a long minute. "I didn't know you had problems with Mom and Dad moving. I thought you were all in on the idea."

"I was, but change is hard. No matter how good the outcome." Reggie pitched the napkin toward the waste basket. It sailed straight and true, landing with a soft swish. "I mean, Mom and Dad couldn't be happier where they are now, but every once in a while, I catch myself thinking about the next big holiday. I have to stop and remind myself that we won't be celebrating it at our old house."

Erin tsked. "I do the same thing." Turning to Michelle, she brought the conversation back to the problem at hand. "Do they know why? Not just your reason for moving here, but that you didn't have a choice—you had to sell the old house?"

Michelle sighed. "I've tried to explain it. I find talking about the situation incredibly difficult to do without painting their father in a bad light. They always kept Allen on a pedestal. I don't want to destroy that image."

Erin pressed her lips together. The movement was one Michelle had seen the blonde make time and time again throughout their long friendship. It usually meant the other girl was keeping something bottled up inside. "Out with it," she ordered.

When Erin still didn't say a word, Michelle watched as the other woman made eye contact with Nina and then Reggie. "The three of you have been talking about the twins amongst yourselves?" she asked, letting the realization sink in. Not that it should come as any big surprise. She'd made no secret of her concerns or how much she wished for a better relationship with her children. "So, what did you come up with?"

Erin's face scrunched, her hazel eyes narrowing. "Well, we think you aren't doing the twins any favors by hiding Allen's faults. Not that dying was his fault, exactly," she added in a hurry. "It's just that he never planned for that possibility, along with a host of other things—how much of your assets he'd have to pour into the new business or how long it would take to get it off the ground." She took a breath. "Or that it might fail completely."

"He was always a dreamer," Michelle admitted wistfully. "A strange trait for an engineer, right?"

"Right," Erin agreed. The skin around her eyes loosened, and her features lost some of their tightness. "But here's the thing. It's important for the twins to know what you've had to face and how you've had to make some very tough decisions since Allen's death. They need to understand that your life bottomed out. Just as important, they need to see that you've bounced back. You didn't let Allen's death destroy you. You're going to be okay. Just like they're going to be okay."

Reggie picked up where Erin left off. "Their father's death was a huge loss. It's going to take time—probably longer than anyone can imagine—for Aaron and Ashley to deal with it."

Michelle blinked. Was Reggie talking about Allen or her own situation? She didn't have more time to mull the question over because Nina had joined the conversation.

"The twins are going to face other hard knocks in life. By watching you, they'll learn that when life knocks you down, you don't wallow. You pick yourself up, dust yourself off, and move on."

"If one door closes, another one opens," Reggie added.

"Right," Erin nodded. "But only if you're looking for it."

"And you have good friends who stick by you through the rough patches, lend you a hand when you need it, and sometimes give you a little push," Michelle finished. She felt tears prick at the corners of her eyes.

They fell silent for a moment before Michelle cleared her throat. Her friends had offered great advice, but none of them had answered her original question. "So do I invite them down or not?" When everyone remained silent, she drummed her fingers lightly against the tabletop. What would she do if Erin, Nina or Reggie turned down her request? She couldn't very well have the twins stay here anyway, not when just the other day, she'd insisted they all had an equal say in running the inn. "If you don't think it's a good idea, it's okay," she said, offering another option. "I can get hotel reservations for the three of us in Destin for the weekend."

"Don't be ridiculous. With all this room"— Erin gestured beyond the kitchen to the rest of the house—"it doesn't make any sense that you'd go somewhere else."

"I don't have a problem with them staying here," Nina said, "as long as they treat you well."

"Look at it this way," Reggie suggested. "Once we open the inn, we're going to have difficult guests from time to time." She grinned. "This will give us a chance to practice our hospitality skills."

"Well, I for one would love to see my god-children." Erin lightly patted Michelle's wrist.

Nina nodded. "Having them here will give me a chance to test out some of the new dishes I'm thinking of adding to the café's menu."

Reggie shrugged. "I could always use an extra pair of hands in the garden if they get tired of sunbathing on the beach."

Michelle laughed. From the time Ashley was two and ice cream had leaked out of the bottom of her cone onto a new dress, she had cut a wide berth around anything messy. As for Aaron, hand him a complicated problem, and he'd design a software program to resolve it. But get his hands dirty? Not so much.

"So it's okay if I invite them down?" she asked, just to be sure.

"As long as they don't interfere with preparations for the open house, I don't see why not," Erin answered for the rest.

The storm had blown itself out while they talked. Michelle smiled. Though the sky remained gray and rain drizzled, she had the feeling better things were on the horizon.

# Seven

## Michelle

Michelle's sensible heels tapped against the concrete steps that led down from the front porch. She gave a cheery wave to Erin, who sat behind the wheel of the big, white SUV. Its motor hummed. Crossing the short distance to the car, Michelle slipped into the passenger seat. As she settled her purse on the floor at her feet, the short black hair on her cream-colored slacks stuck out like a sore thumb.

"How?" she asked. "I haven't seen Mr. Pibbs around. Not once. So how did cat hair end up on my pants?"

"I suspect our resident kitty has been prowling about whenever he gets the chance. I caught him lounging on one of the living-room sofas before I went out for my run this morning. He looked very comfortable."

"Resident kitty." Michelle smiled as she removed the offending cat hair. "That's a good term for him. Once we get the inn up and running, we'll need to make our guests aware of our four-legged resident. In case someone's allergic."

"The next time I update our brochure, I'll add it," Erin said. "Are we all set?"

"I think so." Michelle ran down her mental checklist. Reggie had walked the driveway from one end to the other first thing. They'd heard her using the tractor to dump sand on the particularly muddy parts. She'd assured Michelle the car could make it to the street without getting stuck. With the decision of which vehicle to take made, she and Erin had filled the SUV's storage area with the beautiful gift baskets they'd assembled. She scrolled to the first name on the list of the town council members she'd added to the contacts in her phone. "We're starting with Maggie Henson, aren't we? She said we could catch her at the restaurant before noon." In addition to serving as the town's mayor, Ms. Henson owned and operated Maggie's Diner.

"Sounds good. We've earmarked one basket for Gus, haven't we?"

"We'll stop there last so we can pick up a few things before we head home." Michelle's mouth watered. "I'm looking forward to some more of that sausage." The smoky, spicy links Erin brought home the week before last had disappeared in a flash.

"It was good, wasn't it?" The cellophane around the baskets rustled as Erin drove slowly down a driveway that boasted more bumps than usual, thanks to all the rain. "Nina wants to work some up as an appetizer to serve at the open house."

"That's a great idea," Michelle nodded. "When we visit the businesses in town today, we should keep an eye out for other, local products we can use at the inn." The more they could involve the citizens of Sugar Sand Beach, the better.

"Speaking of businesses, have you driven through town yet?" Erin coasted down the hill toward the gate.

"No, but I'm dying to see it." Michelle pictured the quaint shops and tree-lined streets of some of the smaller towns in Virginia.

"It's not very big," Erin warned.

At the gate, which they'd left open ever since their arrival, Erin turned left toward the main highway. She'd gone less than a quarter of a mile, however, before she turned onto a quiet street that ran from east to west a few blocks away from the beach. Up ahead, the road widened a bit. "Here it is, the thriving metropolis of Sugar Sand Beach," Erin announced with a flourish.

Michelle stared through the windshield. Clusters of birds of paradise and fountain grass filled a center median that ran the length of two city blocks. Anchored on one end by the Sugar Sand Beach Grocery store and a similarly named hardware store at the other, a smattering of businesses and shops sat behind the slanted parking spaces that lined either side of the road. She spotted a barber shop, a hair salon and the community center on one side. Across the street sat a tiny florist shop, as well as a couple of stores that apparently catered to tourists—a shell shop, a souvenir shop, even a surf shop. She smiled at that last one. "Does anyone actually surf in the Gulf?"

Erin headed for the diner midway down the block. "The waves can get pretty big when a hurricane threatens."

"Let's hope we never have to deal with one of those," Michelle said. Huge storms with names like Michael and Andrew and Sandy had wreaked millions of dollars' worth of damage to coastal communities.

"Yeah, let's," Erin agreed. The diner had its own parking lot, and she found an empty space in the shade of a towering oak tree.

"It's surprisingly busy for a weekday morning," Michelle remarked as Erin took one of the gift baskets from the storage compartment. Nearly a dozen cars were parked close to the tree. Some distance away, another group of cars baked in the hot sun. She thought those probably belonged to the employees.

"It's the only restaurant for miles," Erin said. At the entrance, she held the door for Michelle.

Blessedly cool air carried the good smells of bacon, eggs and syrup when they stepped inside. Just beyond the door, an old-fashioned cash register sat on a glass-topped display cabinet that housed a selection of candy bars. Crowded booths lined the exterior walls, where picture windows offered diners a view of the parking lot. A row of four-tops down the center of the restaurant provided additional seating, but those were empty except for one party of four men with deep suntans. Wearing bibbed overalls and baseball caps fitted snugly on their heads, they lingered over coffee. Three or four bustling waitresses dressed in black pants and T-shirts advertising the diner carried loaded trays or took orders throughout the room.

One of them stopped long enough to give Michelle a harried smile. "Sit anywhere you like, darlin'. One of us will be right with you," she said with an accent as thick as the gravy covering the plate of biscuits she carried.

"Um," Michelle started. She'd intended to ask for the owner, but the waitress had hurried to a booth where she plunked down an order.

"I guess we'll sit," Erin said. She headed for the closest empty table.

Within a minute, a different waitress with the same melodic accent arrived to take their order.

"Awww. How purdy," Sally, according to her nametag, gushed over the basket Michelle had lowered onto an empty chair.

"Thanks." She flashed the waitress a warm smile. "We're new to the area and are visiting some of the local businesses to introduce ourselves. I'm Michelle, by the way. And this is one of my business partners, Erin."

"Welcome to Sugar Sand Beach, Michelle. Erin," Sally said, nodding at each of them. "Y'all planning to open a store or something? We sure could use a clothes shop. Other than the thrift store—where you can sometimes get a bargain—the closest place to buy nice things is in Destin."

"I inherited a house not far from here," Michelle said simply. "We'd like to convert it into an inn, and we were hoping to speak with the mayor—Ms. Henson—about our plans. Is she available?"

"Maggie's in the back. Hang on a sec, and I'll get her for you. Meantime, what can I get you?" Sally whipped out an order pad, her pencil ready.

"Just coffee, thanks," Michelle said.

"Two," Erin added.

"Coffee it is," Sally said, slipping the pad into the pocket of the short apron she wore around her waist. "I'll be back in a jiff."

True to her word, their waitress returned seconds later brandishing three thick white mugs in one hand and a carafe in the other. Before she finished pouring, a diminutive white-haired woman wearing one of the restaurant's polos tucked into black slacks emerged from somewhere behind the kitchen area. She made a beeline for their table.

"Hi, folks. I'm Maggie, and welcome to my diner. Sally said you'd like to speak with me about opening a new business in town. Before we go any further, let's get one thing straight— you're not associated with a chain, are you?"

"No, ma'am. We are not," Erin assured her.

"Well, that's good to hear. We probably get one or two inquiries from franchise owners every week. We tell them all the same thing—no chains allowed in Sugar Sand Beach."

Michelle stood and extended a hand. "I'm Michelle Robinson, and this is my best friend and one of my business partners, Erin Bradshaw."

"Pleased to meet you," Maggie said, exchanging the requisite shake.

Their palms grazed just long enough for Michelle to get a quick impression of work-hardened skin and a firm grip before Maggie pulled out the chair next to Erin and sank onto it. She slid the third coffee mug closer asking, "What kind of business did you have in mind?"

"An inn with a café," Michelle answered. She dove into a short explanation. "I've inherited the Simmons property. As you probably know, the house has been sitting vacant for some time. It needs quite a bit of sprucing up. But we're hoping to have it ready for guests in time for the winter tourist season."

"Nancy's old place?" Surprise sent Maggie's eyebrows skyrocketing. "I heard someone satisfied the tax lien. Does Orson know about this?"

"He does." Erin leaned back in her chair. "He wasn't thrilled with the idea."

"I should say not." Maggie tsked. She inclined her head toward one of the windows overlooking the main street. "Orson was born about a mile from where we're sitting right now. Graduated from South Walton County High School along with all the other kids from Sugar Sand. The last year or two, he's been talking about the big housing project he plans to build on the Simmons land—your place now. How it'll bring an economic boost to the community. So no. I imagine he's not happy about you at all."

Michelle's heart sank. It sounded like Orson was one of Sugar Sand Beach's favorite sons. If so, their prospects of even getting their proposal on the town council's agenda—much less approved—were dimmer than she'd anticipated. But she wouldn't throw in the towel. Not when walking away meant giving up on the fresh start Nancy's gift meant for her friends and her. She bought a moment to muster her courage and her thoughts while she spooned sugar into her coffee and gave it a good stir.

"Sugar Sand Beach is a beautiful community," she said at length. "I admit I didn't grow up in this area like Orson did, but in the short time I've been here, I've fallen in love with the area's laid-back atmosphere, its beautiful beaches, the friendliness of everyone I've met. My partners feel the same as I do. What we're proposing is a first-class inn that will provide jobs and attract tourist dollars to the area. And, unlike Orson's plans, those dollars will stay right here in the community because we don't have outside investors—it's just the four of us—and we intend to make Sugar Sand Beach our home."

When Michelle fell silent at last, the mayor and business owner propped her elbows on the table, folded her hands together and rested her chin on them. Michelle couldn't be sure, but she thought the tiniest smile played across the woman's face.

"You sure give an impassioned speech. I'll give you that much," Maggie said at last. "I assume you'll want the council to approve a zoning change?"

"Yes." Michelle nodded. "This project is something I feel very strongly about." To say nothing of the money they'd already spent, money they'd lose if they couldn't open the inn on schedule.

Despite the smile, Maggie shook her head. "The town council meets on the last Tuesday of the month in the Community Center. Our next one is on May 25th. I'm sorry, but it's too late to add your proposal to our agenda for that meeting." The mayor sipped her coffee.

"Oh, that's too bad." Disappointment rippled through Michelle. All their plans for the inn depended on getting the council's approval. They couldn't even pull the permits necessary for some of the repairs without it. "My attorney— Dave Rollins—he told us the council looked favorably on the idea of re-zoning the property for commercial development, but we need their formal approval before we can apply for the licenses to open the inn and the café."

"I know Dave. He's good people. He helped us get our town charter straightened out a few years back…and he did it for free." Maggie idly mopped a wet spot on the table with her napkin. "He's right, though. You won't get anywhere with the county or the state without the council's say-so, and I imagine you'd like to get started as soon as possible?"

"We would." Michelle nodded. They'd already paid off the tax bill. Expenses would continue to mount while they worked on the house. The sooner they could open the doors to the public, the better.

"I tell you what," Maggie said, apparently reaching a decision. "There's an open discussion period at the end of the meeting. I'll give you ten minutes of that time to present your plan. If you can convince the rest of the council that your idea makes sense for Sugar Sand Beach, we'll put it to a vote the following month."

"I'll be there. We all will. I—we—really

appreciate you giving us this chance, Ms. Mayor."

Her tight curls bobbing, the mayor laughed. "Maggie, please. We don't stand on formalities around here."

"Maggie, then." It was Michelle's turn to smile. They'd planned their open house for the weekend before the May council meeting. The timing couldn't be better. "We—Nina, Reggie, Erin and I—we'd love it if you could come to the open house we're holding in a couple of weeks. It'll be a good opportunity for everyone here in Sugar Sand Beach to get to know us and to see a little bit of what we have planned for the inn." She lifted the gift basket from the chair beside her and held it out. "All the details are in here."

"Lovely."

The single word told Michelle it had been worth every bit of effort Nina and Erin had poured into the days of baking cookies and fancy treats, the hours she'd spent arranging the items in the baskets "just so" and the endless times Reggie had re-tied the ribbons, not stopping until they were perfect.

Maggie bent over her gift and drew in a deep breath. "Mmmm. Lemon. My favorite. If it tastes as good as it smells, I'll have to ask your cook for the recipe."

"That'd be Chef Nina," Erin piped up. "She

left a much sought-after position at Café Chez Jacques in Arlington to be a part of our venture. We're very lucky to have her."

A flicker of concern crossed over Maggie's face. Michelle rushed to offer reassurances. "We're starting out very small—five or six tables, primarily for our guests. Breakfast and light lunches until we see how it goes." Of course, they'd love to add a dinner service, but only time would tell if the effort would be profitable.

"Not to worry," Maggie said with a smile. "For years, I've wished someone would open another restaurant in Sugar Sand. People around here deserve a little variety. We all get tired of driving to Destin or Panama City when we want something besides cheese grits or sausage gravy." The woman leaned back in her chair, a speculative look on her face. "You said you *inherited* the Simmons property?"

"Yes. I was Nancy's sole heir." Michelle swallowed. She and Erin had prepared for this line of questioning, but she'd hoped to avoid it.

"Oh. A relative, then." Maggie's gaze narrowed. "Sure took a while for you to come forward. Folks around here just assumed, after one year passed and then another, that one day soon the property would revert to the state. Developers like Orson were lining up to buy it."

Michelle gave her head a sad shake. "I never met Nancy and only heard of her passing six weeks ago. Our families…hadn't stayed in touch." Though attitudes about unmarried women having babies had changed considerably in the forty-five years since Nancy Simmons had given birth, Michelle wasn't going to turn her birth mother into grist for the local rumor mill. Not when the woman had protected her secret until the day she died.

"That's too bad. You missed out on knowing a wonderful woman." Sympathy filled Maggie's face, but Michelle wasn't able to tell whether the feeling was directed at her or her birth mother. "She and I were great friends up through high school. But then that terrible, terrible accident happened. Nancy was so badly injured, she spent months at a rehab center. Somewhere near Miami, I think. She was just a shell of herself when she came home. Started spending more and more time cooped up in that big house of hers. Didn't want to see anyone, not even her friends. We didn't forget her, though. The Ladies Auxiliary ran errands for her. I had the diner send meals over to her on the nights I knew her housekeeper had the day off."

Just then, Sally stopped by their table with

a full carafe of coffee. "Seconds, anybody?" she asked.

"None for me, thanks, Sally." Maggie pushed her chair away from the table. "I've got to get back to work, but you're welcome to stay as long as you'd like. The lunch rush won't start for another hour yet."

Michelle stood. "Thank you for taking the time to talk with us. We need to head out, ourselves. We're planning to stop by and say hello at several of the other businesses in town."

"Well, that's real nice of you. It was sure good meeting you, Michelle. Erin. I'll look forward to seeing you again at the council meeting." Scooping her gift basket from the table, Maggie hurried past the cash register and down a short hall that ran between the kitchen and the bathrooms.

Erin turned to Sally. "How much do we owe for the coffee?"

"Oh, pshaw." The waitress waved the coffee-pot like a magic wand. "It's taken care of." She nodded toward the back of the restaurant, where Maggie had disappeared. "Next time you stop by, y'all be sure and try our cheese grits. They'll change your life." After dispensing that piece of advice, Sally dashed to a booth where she began refilling coffee cups for two diners.

"That went better than I expected in some ways, not as good as I'd hoped in others," Michelle whispered to Erin as they picked their way across the parking lot. "I'm worried about this Orson fellow. Do you think he'll be a problem?"

"I've been thinking he might be." Erin fished in her pocket for the car keys. She clicked the fob. A second later, the lights on Michelle's SUV blinked. "I mean, he's obviously well known around here. So I really thought the mayor would send us packing. But Maggie surprised me when she gave us time to speak at the next council meeting. She didn't have to do that."

"No, she really didn't." Michelle stepped around a puddle left over from yesterday's rainstorm. "I don't think she would have let us present our ideas if she was a hundred percent behind Orson's plan."

"So maybe we have a chance." Erin grinned as she opened the car door and slid behind the wheel.

"Maybe we do." A very good chance to make the Sugar Sand Inn a reality and give Erin, Nina, Reggie and her a second chance at happiness.

# Eight

*Reggie*

Reggie kept the tractor's pace steady as it pulled the attached box blade down one side of the driveway. Thankful for the powerful piece of machinery, she divided her attention between the road ahead and the two-foot steel ripper teeth behind her. The big tines bit into the ground, churning up dirt, grass and gravel. More of the latter than she'd dared hope for filled the tractor's wake. She crossed her fingers, hoping they wouldn't need that extra truckload of stone after all.

Mentally, she reviewed the steps she'd need to take in order to finish the job. For years, cars and trucks going up and down the driveway had compressed the gravel into the dirt or thrown it off to the sides. Her job today was to dig it all back up again, exposing as much of the crushed white rock as possible. To do that, she'd make a couple of passes with the ripper teeth. When the surface of the driveway was nicely churned, she'd raise the steel tines and lower the scraper. Its two wide blades would plow up the gravel and separate it from the loose dirt. She'd have to go back and forth over the driveway at least twice, but by the time she finished, several inches of pretty white stone would cover the drive from one end to the other. She'd make one last pass with the box scraper set at an angle. This would force some of the gravel toward the middle of the road, where it'd form a raised crown. That final touch would keep water from pooling in the center when it rained. If the weather held, she should finish the entire job before nightfall.

Pleased with her progress so far, she scanned the sky for storm clouds, but there weren't any. Yesterday's front had passed on through, leaving behind crystal-blue skies dotted with white puffy clouds. Smiling, she glanced forward.

A half-second later, her smile frozen, she jammed on the brakes. The powerful tractor rocked to a stop. Metal complained and heavy chains jangled as momentum carried the attached box scraper forward. But held in place by powerful steel arms, there was nowhere for it to go. The ripper teeth plowed another inch or two of earth, sending a mix of sand and gravel spilling over the top of the box. Then they settled.

"Whew!" Reggie pulled off the old straw hat she'd found hanging from a peg on the back porch. She mopped her forehead with one arm and wasn't at all surprised when the sleeve of the long-sleeved cotton shirt came away damp. She'd been so focused on what was happening behind her that she hadn't noticed the big pickup truck on the grass up ahead. Or the man who now stood not ten feet in front of the tractor.

Where had he come from?

She swallowed her irritation at having to stop in the middle of her job and took a closer look at the unexpected visitor. All long legs and wide shoulders, he wore a loose T-shirt over jeans that went on forever. He'd pulled the visor of a baseball cap promoting the local hardware store low over his face. His eyes and nose were hidden in shadows, but his lips turned up in a friendly smile.

"Hey!" he called over the noise of the tractor. His lips parted enough to reveal even, white teeth. He nodded to the trail of gravel and dirt behind the tractor. "Good job. I saw you working from the road. Thought I'd stop and lend a hand, but you look like you know what you're doing."

"Thanks. It's not my first rodeo." Reggie settled her hat back on her head.

"You're not from around here, are you?" the stranger asked.

"We moved here from Virginia recently," she said emphasizing the first word. She tilted her head to get a better look at the guy. Was this the usual friendly curiosity they'd encountered everywhere they went since arriving in North Florida? Or did the man want something? He hadn't come any closer, and he wasn't throwing off the kind of vibe that sometimes made the hairs on the back of her neck stand up straight. Still, she was alone and knew Nina wouldn't hear her if she called out. She kept the tractor's motor running.

"I'm Chris. Chris Johnson." Strands of straw-blond hair tumbled onto his forehead when he swept the baseball cap off his head. "I worked for Ms. Simmons back in the day. Since she passed, I've kept an eye on the place for her lawyer—that Mr. Rollins."

"You're the person I need to thank for the excellent shape old Betsy's in?" Feeling more at ease, Reggie powered down the tractor.

"Old Betsy?" The crow's feet around a pair of startling blue eyes crinkled.

Reggie patted the dash. "Well, I had to call her something."

"And here I thought his name was John."

Reggie laughed out loud at the joke. When she quit chuckling, she climbed down to the ground. "Seriously," she said, "you did an awesome job on the vehicles. I was able to get this one started up with just a little bit of tinkering."

"I guess you changed the spark plugs?"

Reggie nodded. "Oiled the cylinders, refilled the fluids, cleaned the ignition contacts. That sort of thing." Now that they were both on solid ground, she judged him to stand a little over six-two, a good seven inches taller than her own five-seven.

"Sounds like you know your stuff."

Reggie felt her face warm at the compliment. She tugged on the hem of the old pair of cutoffs she'd pulled on this morning when running into a Mr. Tall, Dark and *Nice* had been the last thing on her agenda. "I used a tractor just like this one in my last job." At Chris's inquisitive expression, she added, "I worked on the landscaping crew for a big nursery. We mostly planted bushes and trees and laid sod for new housing developments. The work here is a little different but a whole lot more interesting."

"There's always something to do on a place this big. That's for sure." Chris re-settled his cap on his head.

Now, that was a shame, Reggie thought, when the best pair of blue eyes she'd seen in a while retreated into the shadows once more. She shrugged. "I guess I'd better get back to work."

"That driveway won't grade itself." Chris nodded. "Do you know if the owners are home? I was hoping to introduce myself, see if they have any work they want me to do."

"You've already met one of them." She shot him a teasing look. "Reggie Frank," she said with a grin as she yanked off the heavy work gloves so she could give his hand a proper shake. Firm and cool, it did not disappoint. "Michelle Robinson actually owns the property, but the four of us— Michelle, Nina, Erin and I—are all business partners. We're hoping to turn this place"—she gestured behind her to the house—"into an inn."

"It certainly has the room for it." Chris shook his head. "Always did seem a little sad to me that Ms. Nancy lived alone in that big old place. Houses like that are meant to be full of people and laughter."

"We're going to do our best to make that happen," Reggie said. "Listen, I've got to get back to work on this driveway, but if you have some free time day after tomorrow, I'd appreciate it if you could swing by and help me get the pickup truck started. I've messed with it a bit, but I can't get the engine to turn over. It sure would come in handy for hauling supplies and such."

"Sure thing," the man said. "Is ten okay with you? I'll need to drop the baby off at my mom's place on the way."

"The baby?" Reggie sucked in a breath. Instinctively, she retreated a step. Chris might indeed be Mr. Tall, Dark and Nice, but he was also married and thus, off limits. Not that she was interested. She was still married herself, and she didn't see that changing anytime soon, even though hers was a marriage in name only. But until things were officially, legally over between her and Sam—no matter how long that took—she had no business looking for a new relationship.

Still…a baby.

An old yearning stirred in her chest. Knowing she shouldn't pry but unable to stop herself, she asked, "How old?"

"Six months." The shadow of a smile played across Chris's face. "Her name's Hope. My mom takes care of her when I have work to do. Which is why I can't get started before ten."

"That's fine, Chris. I have plenty to keep me busy until then." She thrust her fingers into her work gloves. Much as she'd dreamed and prayed for a child of her own, a baby wasn't in the cards she'd been dealt. "See you tomorrow."

Imagining a grinning, toothless six-month-old with chubby cheeks, Chris's fine blue eyes and straw-blond hair and that divine smell unique to babies, she turned and slowly walked to the tractor. Absently, she rubbed her belly. A baby of her own wasn't in her future. The sooner she accepted that for real, the better.

# Nine

## Michelle

"This is the last one," Michelle said. She signaled for the turn into the parking lot at the Sugar Sand Beach Grocery store.

"Good. I think I have one last smile in me. Any more and I'm afraid my face will freeze solid." Erin's grin softened her complaint. "Besides, I'm ready for some of that sausage."

Michelle's mouth watered. Gus's smoked sausage was *good!* "You have Nina's list?"

"Right here." From her pocket, Erin withdrew a sheet of paper filled with writing. "It sure takes a lot of groceries to keep four people fed."

"Ha!" Michelle laughed. "You should try feeding teenagers. Aaron, especially. When he was younger, I swear that boy ate his weight in potato chips and crackers every day." She steered around a large puddle in the middle of the parking lot.

"Speaking of the twins, what did my god-children say about coming down for Mother's Day?"

Michelle aimed for one of the many open parking spots. "They can't make it." She hurried to add, "Which I completely understand. Mother's Day falls on the ninth, and classes end on the seventh, so I thought the timing would be perfect. I forgot about finals. They're the following week. The kids'll both be cramming like mad." Aaron and Ashley were finishing up their junior year at UVA.

"Okay, but how about when finals are over?"

Putting the car in park, Michelle gave her head another quick shake. "Ashley and a bunch of her sisters are spending the summer at the sorority house. Kappa Kappa Gamma is well-known for the leadership retreats they run for girls at risk. Ashley is next year's team leader. It's a huge undertaking."

"Whew!" Erin whistled. "There's hope for that girl yet."

"I know, right? Who would have thought my daughter would volunteer for such a big project?" She and Ashley might be on the outs right now, but that didn't stop her from being a proud mama.

"And Aaron?"

"He landed an internship with CJX," she said, dropping the name of the well-known engineering firm. "Out of hundreds of applicants, the company only chose ten. The position practically guarantees him a job once he graduates."

"He couldn't very well turn that down."

"No." Her children were learning to stand on their own merits. Wasn't that what every parent hoped for? "Aaron said they'd both try to come for a visit later in the summer."

"Well, that's something to look forward to." Erin unbuckled her seatbelt. "Frankly, I'm kind of glad we'll get past the open house first. We have a lot to accomplish this month."

"True." Though it would all be wasted effort if they couldn't convince the town council to re-zone the property or approve their proposal. She shifted the conversation. "I think it went well with everyone we visited today, don't you?" Word that the mayor had offered to let them speak at the next council meeting must have spread up and down the one and only street in Sugar Sand Beach. Wherever they stopped, business owners and small-town politicians had welcomed them with open arms.

"Cathy was sweet, although I'd have to be pretty hard up to go to her for a cut and color." When they'd stopped by the beauty salon, the beautician had been in the middle of giving a customer's shoulder-length hair a hopelessly out-of-date pixie cut. Plus, Cathy had dyed her own hair a red so bright, it hurt to look at it.

"I may have to let mine grow out. Or find a salon in Destin." Michelle tucked her hair behind one ear. "But Cathy couldn't have been nicer, and she seemed really interested in our plans for the inn."

"Everyone did."

From Matt, who ran the barber shop, to Frank and Ronni, the brother and sister who owned the only hardware store in town, straight on down to tiny Polly Denton, owner of Polly's Posies, Michelle and Erin had been treated to warm Southern hospitality at every stop.

"If things go this well at the council meeting—" Michelle stepped from the car onto the asphalt parking lot.

"Don't say it," Erin interrupted. "You don't want to jinx us."

She giggled, but Erin's remark kept her from saying they'd be a shoo-in. After opening the rear hatch, she lifted the final gift basket from the SUV's storage area and straightened the bow.

"Ready?" she asked as Erin rounded the back fender.

Together, they turned toward the store in time to see a familiar figure exit carrying a cloth sack. "Isn't that Dave Rollins?" Erin pointed with her chin.

"What's he doing in Sugar Sand Beach this time of day?" Michelle tugged at her slacks, smoothing creases that had formed after four hours of climbing in and out of the SUV.

"I don't know. Shopping maybe? It is a grocery store," Erin said with a well-timed elbow jab.

"Ouch. But why here?" Michelle squared her shoulders. "Destin has bigger stores. Didn't you say people come from all over for the sausage? Could that be it?"

"Why don't you ask him?"

"I don't know…" Michelle hesitated. She liked the guy, but she wouldn't want to give him the wrong idea. She wasn't in the market for anything more than a casual friendship.

"Don't look now, but he's walking this way," Erin whispered.

Well, there was nothing for it—she had to say hello. It'd be rude not to. She took a breath. "Hey, Dave," she called when he stopped at the car two parking spots from where she and Erin stood. "What brings you to Sugar Sand Beach in the middle of a workday?"

"Gus and I had a few things to talk over." He set his briefcase and the cloth bag into the trunk of a shiny gray sedan. A warm smile filled the tall man's face. "How about you?"

"We're delivering gift baskets to business owners and members of the town council. We wanted to introduce ourselves before the next meeting." Concerned that they were breaking some kind of rule, Michelle hesitated.

"What a nice, neighborly thing to do." Dave gave the basket with its bright yellow bow an approving glance. "Is that for Gus?"

Erin spoke up. "He's the last one on our list."

"In that case, I'm going to stop at Maggie's for coffee before I head back to Destin. When you're finished here, why don't the two of you join me for a cup?" Dave hit the button on his key fob, and his car's trunk lid lowered.

Suddenly thirsty for some of Maggie's freshly brewed coffee, Michelle turned to her friend. "I think we have time for one cup, don't you?"

Erin replied with a sly smile. "I have too much to do today, but I tell you what." With a quick, deft movement, she plucked the gift basket from Michelle's hands. "Why don't you grab that coffee with Dave while I visit with Gus.

I'll swing by and pick you up when I'm finished."

Not quite sure what to do with her hands now that they were empty, Michelle let them drop to her sides. "I guess it's just you and me," she said, hoping Dave wouldn't be disappointed by the change in plans. To her delight, his expression only brightened.

"If you're sure you don't mind, we'll wait for you at Maggie's, then." Rather than discuss the matter any further, he moved to the passenger side, where he held the door open for Michelle.

"See you in a bit," Erin called, already in motion toward the entrance of the grocery store.

Michelle slid onto the plush, leather seat and took a deep breath to settle her nerves. The barest trace of Dave's aftershave mingled with a new-car smell. She summoned a smile that was far steadier than she felt when Dave took his place behind the wheel.

"Your car looks like you just drove it off the showroom floor. It's new?" she asked, sticking to a safe topic.

"A lease." Dave nodded. The parking lot behind them appeared on a screen when he shifted into reverse. "The firm's accountant insists we trade vehicles every two years. I picked this one up last week."

"It's nice." She started to ask him about the pros and cons of leasing versus buying but stopped herself. That conversation could go on for a while, and she didn't want to pass up the opportunity to learn more about the man responsible for her being in Florida. "So Rollins and Rollins is a family firm. I guess that means you've lived around here your entire life?"

"In Destin, yes. I went to Florida State for my undergrad degree. To the University of Florida for law school. That makes me a bit of a rare breed around these parts. The two schools are bitter rivals."

"So which is it? The Seminole Chop or the Gator Chomp?" She mimicked the motions of each school's mascot. She hadn't lived in Florida long, but with two kids in college, she understood the importance of football.

"Whichever one has the better quarterback." Dave chuckled. "How about yourself? Had you lived in Virginia long?"

"All my life. I met Allen when we were both students at UVA." She took a beat, but the tears that had been her constant companion for a year failed to appear. "He was from Pittsburgh," she continued. "He landed a job with a government contractor straight out of school, so we bought a house in Fairfax, the same town where I'd grown up. I worked in design until the twins came along. After that, juggling child care and work schedules—well, it worked out better for me to stay home with the kids. Aaron and Ashley are juniors at UVA now. If they can swing a break from their studies, they'll be down later this summer."

"They should meet my daughter, Sarah. She's twenty-six and clerking for a judge in Tallahassee."

"Followed her dad into law, did she?" Michelle asked.

"For a few years, I was afraid she'd go into medicine like her mom." Dave's chest puffed out the tiniest bit. "I was ecstatic when she majored in pre-law. One of these days, the sign on the door might be Rollins, Rollins and Rollins, but we'll see. She's young yet. Anyway, if she's home, I'm sure she'd be happy to take Aaron and Ashley to all the hot spots that I, as a father, don't want to know anything about."

She laughed. "I hear you. There are things about my children's lives I'd prefer not to know about, too." Liking his humor, she stole a quick peek at Dave. Tall and broad-chested, he was close to her own age. Maybe a little older, judging from the lines around his eyes and mouth. He had a longish face and a mouth and nose that were neither too large or too small. The gray at his temples looked good on him, giving him that distinguished look some men had.

Wondering how she'd react when she started turning gray, she ran a hand through her own hair. So far, it had retained the glossy black color she'd been born with, but many of her friends had put their beauticians on speed dial the moment they discovered their first gray hair.

At Maggie's, she followed Dave to an empty booth, where he ordered coffee for them both. They talked for a while, filling in the blanks in each other's history the way acquaintances who might become friends did. She learned he and his ex-wife had divorced amicably the year their daughter left for college. His ex had moved to nearby Fort Walton Beach, where she'd remarried a couple of years later. As for his own relationships, Michelle suspected there'd been a few women in his life since then, but for whatever reason, he'd steered clear of commitment.

Talking with Dave came so easily, she soon found herself confessing how adrift she'd felt after Allen's death and how the Sugar Sand Inn had given her a new sense of purpose at a time when she really needed it. "That's why it was so encouraging to talk with the members of the town council this morning. I guess I expected more pushback, but they were all so welcoming and positive about the inn. I'm starting to believe we can actually do this."

"You're right about the people who live here." Dave waited while the waitress refilled their coffee cups. "They'd like nothing better than to see your inn be successful. Especially if it means not letting Orson and his backers gain a toehold in Sugar Sand Beach."

Michelle studied Dave's face. The man was saying all the right words, but something in the way he was saying them made her stomach tighten. "What?" she asked. Did he know something she didn't?

"Just don't underestimate the members of the town council, okay? They exude Southern charm, and some people mistake that for a laissez-faire attitude. Nothing could be further from the truth. They take their responsibilities to Sugar Sand Beach very carefully."

Michelle nodded. She caught his drift. "They need to know we have the resources and dedication to turn the inn into a successful enterprise before they'll give Orson and his housing project the boot."

"Something along those lines, yes." Dave leaned forward, his voice pitched low. "Orson's backers have invested too much time and effort into their project to let it die. I'm sure they have their eye on at least one other Gulf-coast property in case things don't work out for them here in Sugar Sand Beach. Wherever they end up, their project will bring new jobs and a big boost to the local economy."

"So our job is to convince the council members they won't lose out by approving our proposal." Her fingers splayed on the tabletop, she counted off the benefits of opening the inn. "We're here for the long haul. We'll support the local economy, first by buying local and second by hiring local. The area's business owners will benefit from the tourists and out-of-town guests who stay at the inn. We're not here to change the face or character of Sugar Sand Beach but to support it." She looked at Dave. "How do we do that?"

Dave gave the slightest shrug. "Make sure your business plan is airtight. If you're going to tear down any of the outbuildings or erect new ones, include how it'll impact the environment. The council members might have been friendly and welcoming, but they'll protect Sugar Sand Beach's interests with the single-minded purpose of a bottlenose dolphin caring for her young."

Michelle smiled, her eyes crinkling. "That's an odd analogy."

"Live around here very long, and you'll get

familiar with the habits of the sea creatures."

"Erin will, for sure. She's an avid kayaker. In fact, I'm surprised she hasn't pulled Nancy's old kayaks down out of the garage and had them in the water already." When Dave grinned, she decided he had a nice smile. She supposed that came in handy in his line of work. Which reminded her, there was one other thing she'd hoped to talk to him about.

"I'll make an appointment to come into the office so we can discuss this officially, but would you mind if I ask a legal question?"

His smile softened. "You don't need to make an appointment. I'm happy to help."

She slid one hand into her lap and crossed her fingers. She liked Dave. She couldn't deny it. The man had gone above and beyond in taking care of her birth mother's estate. He'd been open and honest about Orson and the tax lien. When the lab results came back, he'd tracked her down at the beach to personally deliver the news that Nancy Simmons was her birth mother. But as much as she enjoyed Dave's company, whether their friendship blossomed or not would depend on his reaction to her plans for the property.

"It's about the house. Well, more than that, actually." She was getting it all jumbled. She took a breath and sorted things out. "Erin, Nina and

Reggie are putting everything they have into the inn, and I want them to have a real stake in our venture. I think the four of us need to form a partnership or a corporation—I'm not sure about the correct legal term. But once that's done, I intend to transfer the entire estate into it. What do you think?"

She studied Dave's reaction closely for any sign that his friendship might be based on her inheritance. He seemed interested in her, but was he even more interested in her land? She'd done her research. Even without Orson's offer waiting in the wings, she knew five acres of beachfront property would bring a pretty penny. Her pulse raced. When Dave looked up from stirring his coffee, she held her breath.

"Well, of course. We can certainly do that," he said, putting her doubts to rest. "Do you want everything divided equally? Or do you want to retain a majority stake?"

"Equal partners," she said without hesitation. "Though we may have to work around Reggie for the time being. She's going through a nasty divorce."

"Ah…yes. I can see where that might be a problem. You wouldn't want the ex to have any claim on the property. I'll look into it, but I'm sure we can find a way to safeguard her interest." He sipped his coffee. "Aren't she and Erin sisters?"

"They are." Michelle nodded. That was another thing Dave had going for him. He paid attention. She might have mentioned the connection between Erin and Reggie the first time they met, but she hadn't expected him to remember it.

"If their relationship is sound, the easiest solution would be to assign Reggie's portion to her sister for the time being. Then, once the divorce is final, Reggie could 'buy' it back from Erin," he said, enclosing the word in air quotes.

"That's legal?"

A look of mock horror crossed Dave's face. "I wouldn't suggest it otherwise."

A heady mix of mirth and relief bubbled up from her midsection. She gave Dave one of her best smiles. "So you don't have any objections to splitting the ownership up between us?"

"Why would I?" Confusion clouded his blue eyes. "It's your property. What you do with it is up to you."

"Thanks," Michelle said. Reaching across the table, she gave Dave's hand a light squeeze. As her fingers touched his, a comforting warmth spread up her arm and filled her chest. "It's good to have a friend like you."

Through the plate glass window over their

booth, she spotted her SUV pulling into the parking lot. "Erin's here. I'd better go so I don't keep her waiting." She paused. "I'll call you in a couple of weeks, and we can work out some of the details. Okay?"

"Actually, I'll be in Sugar Sand on Wednesday to meet with a client. I should have a preliminary agreement for you to look over by then. If you'd like, I'd be happy to review your business plan, too. We could meet here for lunch and go over everything."

"I'd like that very much." How much surprised her.

"Till next week, then," he said, standing as she gathered her purse and slid out of the booth. "You go ahead. I'll be right behind you." He signaled for their waitress and the check. "I need to get back before my groceries spoil. I bought some sausage while I was at Gus's."

As she crossed the parking lot toward her car, Michelle smiled to herself. Things were definitely looking up in Sugar Sand Beach, and with any luck, they'd have sausage for supper, too.

# Ten

## Reggie

*R*eggie turned the key in Nancy Simmons's old pickup truck. She heard a soft click, followed by the sound of birds chirping in the trees. Other than that, nothing.

"Shoot," she swore softly. She'd done all the right things—changed the filters, replaced the battery and spark plugs, added new fluids, but nothing worked. The old pickup still refused to start, and she was fresh out of ideas.

Maybe something would come to her while she checked on the ATVs, she thought. Earlier, she'd drafted Erin's help in pushing the two smaller vehicles outside. The long battery cables attached to one of them would, hopefully, charge it up and get it roadworthy. The other, though, was gas-powered and would require a little more maintenance—and a full tank—before they could get any use out of it.

She slid from the truck's bench front seat. Skimming past the running board, her sneakered feet landed on the concrete floor of the garage. She needed to get the truck up and running. The vehicle would come in handy for chores on the five acres surrounding the inn. But whatever was wrong with it had her completely baffled.

She cut in front of the fender just in time to spot Chris walking around the corner of the house. She suppressed a groan. The man was fast making a habit of catching her at her worst. Intending to change before he got here, she'd stepped into a raggedy pair of shorts and pulled a wrinkled T-shirt over her head this morning. Her hair was a disaster. Knowing she'd be working in the garage, she'd secured the loose curls into a messy topknot. But at some point in her struggles with the truck, the elastic had popped. To keep her hair out of her face, she'd swept most of the strands into a baseball cap. The rest were all over the place. And she couldn't shove them back where they belonged, not with grease on her hands. She grabbed a rag from her back pocket and scrubbed at her fingers.

"Good morning," she called once Chris had walked within hailing distance. As he had yesterday, he wore a loose T-shirt over jeans. He grinned from beneath the frayed brim of a well-worn cap, and she caught a glimpse of a toothy smile.

He raised his hand in greeting. "'Morning."

"You're early." She'd expected him around ten and had planned to duck into the house and freshen up a bit before he got here. No chance of that now.

"Mom swung by and picked up Hope. I was able to leave the house a little earlier than I'd planned. Had to promise her I'd come back with lots of good gossip." His face scrunched into a stricken expression. "That's not what I meant. It's just…it's been a while, and she's chomping at the bit to find out all about the new neighbors."

"Tell her to stop by. We won't bite. We'd love to meet her." Reggie tucked the rag into her pocket. "You're both coming to the open house, aren't you?"

"She wouldn't miss it, but I'll have to take a rain check. I don't leave Hope with babysitters. Not yet, leastways."

"Bring her along. I'm sure there'll be other kids here." Deliberately, she ignored the tightness that spread through her midsection whenever the subject of babies came up. Chris was doing her a solid by helping with the pickup today. Inviting him—and his daughter—to the open house was the least she could do to repay him.

"Thanks. I might swing by with her for a bit." He lifted his chin toward the gated entry. "Meant to tell you, the driveway turned out real nice."

Reggie felt her face warm. It had been a long time since a man had offered her a compliment. Her bosses at Green Acres Nursery hadn't been big on stroking the egos of the landscape crew. As for Sam, he was more likely to point the finger than give her a high-five. She cleared her throat. "I was glad we didn't need to bring in another load of gravel."

"Nah. There's plenty. It just needed diggin' out. I'm sorry as I can be I didn't get around to doing it before you got here. The last few months have been…" He paused and seemed to be searching for the right word. "Hectic. But it's done now. You shouldn't have to work on it again for some time."

"The tractor did all the work." And she was glad for it. Like Michelle, she hadn't relished the thought of digging up the drive and raking the gravel by hand.

Chris scanned the backyard, his gaze lingering

on neatly trimmed hedges and flower beds no longer choked with weeds. He whistled. "Somebody's been busy. I haven't seen the shrubs around here look this good in ages. Ms. Nancy, she liked her flowers. She'd be happy to see the house open and spruced up again."

The man was chock full of compliments, wasn't he? Reggie steered the conversation away from herself. "That reminds me. Did we thank you for taking down the shutters? And do we owe you for that work?"

Chris tossed both hands into the air. "Don't worry about it. I couldn't abide the thought of y'all movin' into a hot, dark house. The panels are all stacked in the toolshed for when you need 'em."

"Let's hope that won't be for a while."

"Sooner rather than later, I'm afraid. Hurricane season rarely passes without at least one good blow." Chris glanced over her shoulder toward the garage. "Truck still won't crank?"

Reggie scuffed one foot, kicking up a small cloud of sand. "No, and I've tried everything."

"Did you make sure the battery took a charge?"

She shook her head. "I bought a new one." She'd found the old battery safely stored on the work bench. Though it might have charged up just fine, she dared not trust it. Chances were, it'd fail on her at just the wrong moment. "I changed the oil and fuel filters, cleaned the air filter. Added all new fluids. Checked the wiring harness…" She went down the list.

He nodded his approval. "You got the tractor started, so you obviously know your way around an engine. But sometimes two heads are better than one. Let's see if we can put ours together and solve this mystery."

Trailing Chris on the way to the garage, Reggie stopped in mid-stride. Last winter she'd gone to Sam with a similar sad tale when the engine of her own truck wouldn't turn over. He'd given her an earful of caustic comments, most of them centered on his view that car repairs were men's work. Not that he knew one end of a crescent wrench from another. Or how to do anything more than call for roadside assistance when he ran out of gas. But Chris hadn't reacted that way at all.

"You forget something?" the man in question called from the entrance to the garage.

"Nope. Just thinking about what I might have overlooked." Which wasn't a lie, exactly, even though what she was thinking about had nothing to do with the pickup truck. Lately she'd been thinking there'd been an awful lot of problems she'd overlooked in her marriage. Like how whenever things didn't go his way, Sam usually found some way to make it her fault. And how, like a fool, she'd accepted the blame. Well, enough of that. The days when she'd accept responsibility for every little wrinkle in life were over. She dusted her hands on the seat of her shorts and hurried to catch up with Chris.

"Will it crank at all?" Chris leaned over the open hood.

"Nope."

"And you've checked the spark plugs," he said, without a hint of doubt in his tone.

"Replaced them." She'd driven to the closest auto parts place yesterday after dinner.

"Have you tried jumping it?"

"Yeah. The engine didn't even sputter."

"I wonder if they sold you a bad battery. You got it at Buy Right Auto Parts in Destin?" Chris wiggled the wires connected to the terminals.

"Yeah."

He shook his head. "I know the owner. Norman's pretty good about checking the charge when he sells a battery."

"We put it on the tester," she confirmed. "All green lights across the board."

Chris resettled his baseball cap. "Probably not the battery, then. Not the spark plugs, 'cause you replaced them. The fluid levels all look good. I'm pretty sure I drained the tank. You filled it up?"

"Oh, yeah. The gas tank was bone-dry." She'd been glad of that, since regular gas began to break down in as little as three months. If the tank hadn't been emptied, getting the truck back on the road would have taken a lot more time and effort, to say nothing of the expense.

Chris tinkered for a bit, repeating all the steps Reggie had already taken. At first, concerned that he'd criticize her work, she stiffened. She quickly relaxed when Chris threw out compliments with each motion.

"Yep. That's right," he muttered to himself as he examined the distributor cap.

"You did a good job of tightening these spark plugs. Not too tight. Not too loose," he added a minute later.

At last, he pulled his head out from beneath the hood. "Well, I'm stumped," he said, his hands on his hips. "Looks like you've covered all the bases. It's a mystery to me why it still won't start."

Air seeped from between Reggie's lips. She'd fretted that Chris would find something wrong with her work. Instead, his positive comments had boosted her self-confidence. Trusting him to give her a straight answer, she asked, "Got any idea where we go from here?"

"Good question. I don't rightly kn—" Chris's blue eyes narrowed into a squint. "Wait a minute. Wait a minute," he whispered, obviously talking to himself. He removed his baseball cap and ran a hand through his hair. "It's gotta be electrical, right? The battery checks out. Connection's good. Spark plugs, too. Spark plug wires, all new. That leaves…that leaves…" His eyes opened. He pinned her with a questioning look. "What about the wire that runs from the coil?"

In a flash, he was under the hood again, one hand reaching for the thick, black line.

"Wait a sec!" Reggie called out.

But her warning came too late.

"Yikes!" Chris jumped. His head banged against the underside of the hood. "Yowzah!" Shaking the fingers of his right hand, he stepped away from the truck.

"Are you okay?" Reggie's heart leapt to her throat. Had he hurt himself?

"Yeah, yeah." Chris removed his hat and rubbed his head.

Reggie breathed a sigh of relief when no blood stained his fingers. He'd given his head a good bonk, but at least he hadn't cut it.

"Leave it to me to get shocked and knock myself unconscious on the same day." Chris laughed to himself.

"Glad it didn't quite come to that. Do you want some ice?" She watched as he closed his eyes and she got her first good look at long, sooty eyelashes. She knew some women who'd pay a fortune to have lashes like that. She swallowed and forced herself to focus on the truck.

"Nah. I'm fine. No harm done."

Relieved, she asked, "So, what's wrong?"

"The wire from the distributor cap to the coil is just hanging there by a thread. Not enough juice is getting from Point A to Point B to start the engine. But there's enough to give you a nice jolt if you grab it."

Reggie's face heated for the second time in the last hour, but this time, shame stained her cheeks. "I'm so sorry. I should have caught that."

"Not your fault. I missed it, too." Chris resettled his cap on his head. "Probably a squirrel nibbled on it. They'll chew on anything. We'll need to replace that wire. I don't suppose you picked up a new one in Destin?"

She shook her head. Wire-eating rodents hadn't factored high on her list of concerns while she shopped. She patted her pockets for the keys to her own pickup before she remembered that Erin and Nina had borrowed it first thing this morning. That left Michelle's SUV. She was sure her friend wouldn't mind if they took the big Escalade, but the round trip would take at least an hour. Time she didn't want to waste.

She reached for her phone. "Erin and Nina were going to that big box store in Destin. Let me see if I can catch them before they head back."

When Erin answered on the first ring, Reggie made quick work of explaining what they needed and was relieved when her sister said they'd stop at the parts place on their way. After thanking her, Reggie turned to Chris.

"Caught them just in time. They were loading the car and getting ready to come home. They'll stop for the part on the way. Should be here within the half hour."

"Good to hear. I'll call Norman. Have him set what we need aside to save them some time." After placing the call, Chris leaned against the truck as if he wasn't in any hurry to go any-where.

Curious about the man who'd given up his morning to help her out, Reggie asked, "You want a glass of tea? Or some water? We could sit on the porch and wait. If you don't have something else you need to do, that is."

A slow, easy smile worked its way up Chris's face until it reached his eyes. "I wouldn't turn down a glass of tea." His brow furrowed. "It is sweet, isn't it? I keep forgettin' y'all are from up north."

"Hey." Reggie made a face. "I resent that. We're all from Virginia. Last I heard, that was well south of the Mason/Dixon line."

"Oh yeah?" Chris challenged. "When you go into a restaurant in Vuh-gin-ya and you order tea, does it come already sweetened?"

"Well, no." No matter how many packets of sugar she poured into it, Reggie could never get it to taste right.

"I rest my case." Chris folded his arms across his wide chest.

"You got me there," Reggie admitted. "But when in Rome...Nina fell in love with the tea we got at a fried-chicken place on the way down here. She's been tinkering with a recipe, trying to get hers as good as theirs."

"I guess I just volunteered to be her guinea pig, then." Chris pushed himself off the truck.

Thankful that they'd all pitched in the other day and treated the porch to a thorough cleaning, Reggie suggested, "Why don't you go on round to the front of the house. I'll meet you there."

She made a beeline for the back entrance. Out of the corner of her eye, she caught a quick glimpse of Chris's long strides as he headed for the other side of the house. The man did cut a nice figure, she thought as she stomped and scraped her boots on the door mat. Her focus shifted to the job at hand, though, when she stepped into the kitchen. After opening and closing several cabinets, she finally located the glasses. She took two down and filled them with ice. Grabbing the tea from the top shelf of the fridge, she gave the pitcher a quick stir before she poured the caramel-colored liquid over the ice. While she was at it, she whispered a prayer that this was one of Nina's better attempts at recreating the drink that was standard fare throughout the South.

"If it's good, I'll take full credit," she said, handing one of the tumblers to Chris a minute later.

"And if it's not?" A twinkle sparkled in his blue eyes.

"Then it's all Nina's doing. She's been experimenting, trying to find just the right mix. She made one with agave syrup the other day. That was...interesting." Reggie turned up her nose. She hadn't liked the beverage's earthy aftertaste.

Chris took a long pull from his glass. "Not bad," he pronounced. "For a Northerner. Tell her to boil the sugar with a cup or two of water to start. It'll keep the sugar from sinking to the bottom."

Reggie sipped and tasted. This attempt was a definite improvement over the agave, but Chris was right. It wasn't sweet enough. She held her glass up to the light. A few white crystals had accumulated at the bottom. "Sounds like you're quite the iced tea expert."

"Had to be. My wife was from Boston. She drank her tea hot, with milk. No sugar. I had to get my mom to teach me how to make it myself."

Reggie's brows knitted. She'd assumed Chris was married, so the reference to his wife came as no surprise. But he hadn't mentioned her before and, from the way he talked, she was no longer in the picture. Sensing he had a story to tell, she asked, "From Massachusetts, huh? How'd you two meet?"

"She was down here visiting her aunt in Fort Walton Beach. They went out for a Sunday drive, and their car got a flat. I stopped to help out." Ice cubes clinked against the glass as he shifted his drink from one hand to another. "We had a—I guess you'd call it a whirlwind courtship. We got married six weeks later."

"Love at first sight, huh?" She wondered what that was like. She and Sam had been together for three years before they tied the knot. As she'd recently discovered, though, not even a lengthy courtship guaranteed success for the marriage.

But the day was too pretty and the company too interesting to dwell on her troubles. Determined to focus on the positives, she smiled. "She'll come with you to the open house, won't she? Your wife, I mean. I'll look forward to meeting her."

Chris set his drink down on the glass-topped wicker table. "I'm sorry. I keep forgetting you're new to the area. 'Round here, everybody's up in one another's business so much, I just take for granted everyone knows." He stared past the sea grass and scrub pines to the beach. In a voice devoid of emotion, he said, "Connie, she died when Hope was born. The placenta separated. We barely got her to the hospital. They rushed her into surgery, but they couldn't stop the bleeding."

"Oh! I am so sorry. I had no idea." Reggie's heart took the express elevator to the basement. She clamped one hand over her mouth. Sensing Chris needed to talk about losing his wife, she sat quietly while the story of a harrowing ambulance ride and what followed poured out of him.

At last, he took a breath. Like a man coming out of a trance, Chris blinked. He mopped his face with his hands. "It's been rough. Connie and me, we hadn't known each other that long. Less than a year. But what we had was real, you know? There's days when I wake up and I can't believe she's gone. That Hope will never get to know her mother. Connie was—we were both so happy about the baby."

He drained the rest of his tea in long gulps. Sheepish, he stared at Reggie. "I don't know why I told you all that. It's not something I ever talk about. I never saw the point of rehashing what everybody already knows."

"Maybe that's why," she answered softly. "You needed to talk, and here I was, someone who didn't know your story." She paused. "What about Hope? Was she okay?"

A faint smile traced across Chris's face as he nodded. "She's the one blessing to come out of this. Though I'm not sure what I would have done if my mom hadn't been here to help me out. She's been a godsend. And that little girl, I just want to do right by her. She's got this sweet little grin. And when she laughs, you just can't help but laugh right along with her. She's the light of my life."

"Of course she is." When the conversation drifted from Chris's late wife to his daughter, Reggie leaned forward. "Do you have pictures?"

Chris nodded and patted his back pocket. She held out her hand. "Let me see."

Thirty seconds later, her throat tightened as she paged through dozens of photos on Chris's phone. "Oh, my goodness. What a cutie," she said, staring down at images of a toothless cherub who sported a mile-wide grin. In every picture, the baby wore a sweet little outfit with a matching, flowered headband that held her few sparse curls in place. Her fleshy arms and plump legs looked as if they were in perpetual motion. "I bet she keeps you busy."

"She doesn't crawl yet, but she scoots. Fast. I don't know how I'll keep up with her once she starts walking." Paternal pride filled Chris's voice.

"Is she a good baby?" she asked, even though she knew the question was ridiculous. There was no such thing as a bad baby.

Chris nodded. "Started sleeping through the night when she was just two weeks old. The only times she gets fussy is when her diaper needs changing or she's hungry. How about yourself? You got kids?"

The question punched Reggie square in the gut. A fresh wave of longing for what she'd never have rolled over her. Her breath turned ragged. Abruptly, she handed Chris's phone back to him, rose from her chair and retreated a few steps. At the porch railing, she grasped the top rung so hard she thought it might splinter in her grip.

"You all right?" Chris's voice held a note of concern. "Did I say something wrong?"

"No. It's not you." Struggling to catch her breath, Reggie shook her head. Chris was a relative stranger, yet she felt comfortable around him. Given the circumstances, she thought they might become friends. And friends were honest with one another, weren't they? Turning to face him, she leaned against the porch railing.

"My husband and I are getting a divorce."

"I'm sorry to hear—"

She waved him off. "We had our problems. Our marriage died a long time ago. Only I didn't realize it at the time. The longer we're apart, though, the more I can see I was the only one hanging on. But we wanted a baby. Children. A family." She looked down, refusing to meet Chris's eyes. "We tried for years. Saw all the specialists, did all the treatments. But nothing worked. I couldn't get pregnant. In the end, that was a deal-breaker and he left me. It still stings when I see someone else's child and realize I'll never have one of my own."

"You can't be that old," Chris protested. "You still have time, don't you?"

It was sweet of him to say that, but, sadly, she shook her head. "This divorce is probably going to drag out for a while. I know there are people who would just jump back into the dating pool now—and that's fine; they have to do what's right in their own minds—but I don't believe in starting a new relationship before I've put the old one behind me. By the time that happens, though, well, the risks go up with every year that passes."

"And here I was, bragging on my little girl. You must think I'm heartless." Chris gave his head a slow, sad shake.

"Not at all. You didn't know. Like with you and Connie, this isn't something I tell just anyone." Only Sam and her doctors knew the whole story. None of her girlfriends knew. Why, she hadn't even told Erin. "Besides, you've got your own cross to bear."

A plume of dust rose over the slight rise that stood between the house and the main road. Reggie straightened. "Looks like Erin and Nina are back with the part we need for the truck."

Just in time, too. Before Chris hightailed it out of here like his sanity depended on it. She wouldn't blame him if he did exactly that. He'd just lost his wife, for Pete's sake. He was doing his level best to raise his motherless child on his own. Her troubles paled in comparison. He didn't need to hear them, much less try to shoulder them.

"What's life without a little misery?" Chris slipped his cell phone into his back pocket. He leaned against the chair cushions, his long legs crossed at the ankles. "It's what makes the good times even sweeter."

"Yeah. I guess it does." Reggie took a minute to think about what Chris had said. She hadn't exactly looked at life that way before, but it made sense. When she was little, she'd had to eat her broccoli to get dessert. Her pediatrician had always administered vaccines or vile-tasting medicine before she doled out lollipops. And, after enduring Sam's constant put-downs, Reggie definitely savored the compliments her friends and Chris had given her lately. She looked up at the man, who'd stood as the pickup truck crested the small hill. "I like the way you think, Chris," she said. "It puts a different slant on life's ups and downs."

She would have said more, but her truck pulled to a stop near the front steps. Her sister and Nina hopped out. Reggie made the necessary introductions. She eyed the bed of the truck. Lumps and bumps jutted up from beneath a waterproof tarp that Erin was untying.

"Geez. Did you leave anything in the store for the other customers?" she asked.

"Not much," Nina said with a grin. "Now that we've scrubbed the kitchen from top to bottom, I'm eager to start trying out recipes for the café. Besides, you know how much I love a full pantry."

Erin looked up from her task. "Want to give us a hand unloading all this?"

Chris, who'd descended the front steps to shake hands with the new arrivals, made a show of flexing his arm muscles. "Where do you want it?"

Erin straightened. "Nina, why don't you head into the kitchen. You can tell the rest of us where to put things. Reggie, Chris and I will bring everything inside."

"Sounds good." Nina trooped up the steps.

With Chris's help, Reggie and Erin managed to unload the truck and get everything stored away to Nina's satisfaction in a little less than a half hour. It took another thirty minutes for Reggie and Chris to replace the old wiring in the truck in the garage. At last, Reggie climbed into the driver's seat, crossed her fingers and twisted the key in the ignition. The engine caught, coughed once or twice and settled into a smooth rumble.

"Hooray!" Reggie yelled through the open driver's-side window. She gave Chris a thumbs-up. Leaning out, she asked, "Want to take it for a test drive?"

"Sure." He closed the hood and stood back, surveying the area for any tools they might have left out. Satisfied that there were none, he joined Reggie in the cab. "Where to?"

"Let's see if she makes it to the gate and back. I don't want to take her out on the road until I get new tags for her."

"Hadn't thought of that. Though I doubt the sheriff or his deputies would give you a ticket if you explained what you were doing."

"You're probably right. Still…" She didn't want to get off on the wrong foot with the local police force.

A couple of trips up and down the graveled driveway convinced them both the truck was roadworthy. They'd just finished a third round trip when Chris checked his watch.

"It's about lunchtime. I'd better be shoving off."

Though she wished he'd stick around for a while longer, Reggie turned to him. "Thanks for all your help this morning. I'm not sure I'd have found that bad wire on my own."

"Nonsense." Chris's gaze bore into hers. "It was just a matter of time till you zapped yourself." He grinned.

"Thanks for taking one for the team," Reggie said, laughing.

Chris stopped when he was halfway out of the vehicle. "Call me if you need any help around the place."

"I'm sure we will." Not only had Dave Rollins recommended Chris, she liked him. She thought the others did, too. "We have a list of repairs a mile long."

She waited until he climbed into his own truck and headed out before she drove the pickup around to the garage. Cutting through the kitchen a few minutes later, she heard Nina humming a happy tune while she organized the spice cabinet. Reggie rinsed out the glasses she and Chris had used. His, she put into the dishwasher, but she kept hers and took it to the fridge.

"Chris suggested boiling the sugar and water together next time you make another batch of tea," she said, taking the pitcher from the top shelf. "He said that's the way his mom taught him to do it."

"A simple syrup?" Nina lowered a jar of paprika to the counter. She tapped her upper lip with one finger. "Why didn't I think of that?" She glanced out the window, where the dust was still settling over the driveway. "He's awfully cute. He help you get that old truck going?"

"Yeah." She frowned at the memory. "He got quite a jolt when he grabbed a frayed wire."

"And he still stuck around to help out?" Nina's head canted.

"Like pretty much everyone we've met in Sugar Sand Beach, he's a nice guy. We should hire him to help us with some of the bigger jobs around here."

"We can talk about it at our next house meeting, but I don't see why not. Just..." Nina's voice drifted off.

"What?" Reggie frowned.

"Just be careful. I wouldn't want to see you get involved on the rebound. That kind of relationship never ends well." Her motions deliberate, Nina lined up the remaining spice bottles on the counter.

Reggie took a minute to think while she poured her tea. When she worked at Green Acres, she'd developed an easy give-and-take with her male co-workers. She'd known the names of their wives and children, whose kid played Little League, which ones were better at soccer. Once a week, the whole crew ate lunch together at whatever sub shop was closest to the job they were working on. But that's as far as those relationships had gone. She wasn't looking for anything more than that with Chris, was she?

The plastic wrap from a new set of salt and pepper shakers sat discarded on the counter.

Reggie swept it into the trash can. "You don't have to worry about Chris and me," she said after giving the matter some thought. "It'll take the better part of a year before my divorce is final. If not longer. Till it is, that part of my life is definitely on hold." She let that sink in for a second before she told Nina the rest of the story. As Chris had pointed out, everyone else in Sugar Sand Beach knew about his late wife. Her friends deserved to hear about it, too. If for no other reason than so they wouldn't fall prey to foot-in-mouth disease like she had. She took a breath and plunged on.

"Chris is a new widower. Lost his wife in childbirth six months ago. He's still grieving. Plus, he's a single dad with a baby to raise." She held up her hands like stop signs. "Even if I was interested—and I'm not—it'll be years before he's ready for any kind of relationship again."

And she was okay with that.

Reggie spent the afternoon thinning the hostas and the weedy clumps of birds of paradise near the front gate. She wanted the entrance to be perfect, as it would be the first thing visitors saw when they arrived at Sugar Sand Inn. She made good progress, and by the time the sun rode low in the western sky, the plants no longer looked bedraggled and wild. Plus, by saving the best of the overgrowth, she amassed a good supply of hostas to replant elsewhere.

Ready to call it a day, she loaded the salvaged plants into the truck bed along with an assortment of rakes, shovels, and clippers. Her years in the landscaping business had taught her the folly of leaving her equipment behind or assuming it would be right where she left it when she returned the next day. Only after she accounted for every hoe, spade and pair of gloves did she slip behind the wheel of the old pickup truck. She cranked the engine and smiled when it roared to life on the first try. She made a mental note to thank Chris for his help again the next time she saw him.

The sun had slipped below the horizon before the hostas rested peacefully under a blanket of damp newspaper on the floor of the gardening shed. The birds were issuing their night calls by the time all the tools had been thoroughly rinsed. She had just watered her special project behind the shed when her cell phone buzzed. Expecting Nina's nightly call to supper, she wrestled the device from her back pocket.

"I'll be right in." She rounded the corner of the shed without checking the screen. "What's on the menu?" Not that she cared. Whatever it was, she trusted Nina to make something tasty. Which was good. She'd worked up quite an appetite.

"Where are you, Regina?"

At the sound of Sam's cold voice in her ear, she lost her grip on the watering can. It hit the ground with a clatter.

"What on earth is all that racket? Are you running all over town while I'm working hard to earn a living?"

"Sorry. So sorry. I dropped..." She stopped herself. She didn't owe Sam an explanation or an apology. She hadn't been able to give them a child, but he was the one who'd walked out on their marriage. She took a steadying breath, picked up the can and returned it to the work-bench in the shed. "What do you want, Sam?"

"Well, if you must know, I want you to come home. I want to give our marriage another chance."

"Say what?" Of all the words that could have come out of Sam's mouth, "I want you to come home" were the last ones she'd expected. She was prepared for another demand that she sign the separation agreement. Or to hear him rant about her lawyer and the fact-finding mission that had uncovered Sam's secret bank account.

But asking her to give their marriage another try? Never.

"Okay. I deserved that," Sam said sounding impatient. "I've been a jerk. I'm not proud of it, but you knew what I was like when you married me. I haven't changed. But I—I miss you. Leaving like I did was a mistake. I see that now. And I—I want you to come back."

It hadn't been so long ago that she'd longed to hear Sam say those very words. But something in his delivery put her on edge. She bit her lower lip while she tried to put her finger on what was bothering her.

"We don't have a home to come back to," she pointed out in an effort to buy some time while she figured out what he really wanted. "We gave up the apartment. I sold most of my half of the furniture. The rest I brought with me to Florida."

"As soon as you get here, we'll start looking for a new place," he said as if she'd already agreed to his plan. "I have some money set aside. But, apparently, you already know that. We'll use it for a down payment. We could get a townhouse in the District. With a yard where you could have a garden. How would you like that?"

Reggie found a square of bare drywall and leaned against it. Did he really not know her at all? She'd never wanted the big house, the fancy cars, the memberships at the country club. All she'd ever wanted was a baby. When Sam said they didn't have enough money for the expensive fertility treatments, she'd scrimped and saved and worked double shifts and weekends to pay for them. It hadn't been enough, and they'd ended up with a pile of credit-card debt. Yet all the while he'd been holding out on her, building himself a healthy nest egg. Now he expected her to believe he'd been saving to buy them a house? Ridiculous. There had to be another reason behind his sudden desire to reconcile.

"We could barely afford our apartment. How on earth could we manage a place downtown?" Housing prices inside the Beltway, the highway that circled the nation's capital, were out of sight. Completely out of reach for a lowly associate attorney. Even one with a secret savings account.

"Didn't I tell you?" Sam asked, sounding pleased with himself. "I'm up for a big promotion. They've offered me a junior partnership. We'll be able to afford a nice place. Not that dump where we were before. In the meantime, we can stay at the firm's condo until we find what we're looking for. Dick says we can stay here as long as we want."

A sudden chill swept through Reggie. "You discussed our divorce with Mr. Grominsky?"

"Well, yeah. Of course." He brushed the comment aside. "We had lunch the other day."

*Really.* She'd met the senior partner while Sam was interviewing with Shorter and Grominsky. Over dinner at the man's country club, Dick had boasted about his own twenty-plus years of married bliss. He'd talked at length about the importance of family. She'd sometimes wondered if that conversation had prompted Sam to propose a week later. Or if the ring she wore on the third finger of her left hand had anything to do with the position Sam had landed shortly after they announced their engagement. It seemed strange for him to choose Dick, of all people, to turn to about their marital problems.

*Unless...*

She closed her eyes while all the pieces of the puzzle slid into place. Sam hadn't said he loved her. Or that he couldn't live without her. In fact, he hadn't shown any concern for her or for her feelings at all. So far, the conversation had all been about what he wanted, what he needed. She'd bet money that it hadn't been his idea to discuss the breakup of their marriage with his boss, either. No. It was far more likely that Dick had gotten wind of the impending divorce and given his young associate a firm reminder that rising junior partners at Shorter and Grominsky respected the sanctity of marriage. A messy divorce was just bad optics.

"You should see my new office," Sam continued, apparently without noticing her silence. "It's twice the size of the one I have now. And with my new salary, you can quit your job. Maybe do volunteer work like the other wives."

"No. I don't think so."

"You want to go on mowing other people's grass in the summer? Shoveling snow in the winter?"

The disdain in Sam's voice made her skin crawl. "I've moved to Florida," she reminded him. "We don't have snow down here."

"Oh, come on, Regina. I heard about this bed and breakfast place you and your friends want to open. You don't honestly believe you'll make a go of it, do you? Do you have any idea how many new businesses fail in the first two years? Almost half. A smart person would cut their losses and get out now."

Reggie closed her eyes. Sam was wrong. She and her friends had worked their tails off the past few weeks, and their efforts were paying off. They still had hurdles to clear—getting the town council to rezone the property was high on that list—but if all went well, the Sugar Sand Inn would welcome its first paying guests in time for the busy tourist season.

"You're wrong," she told him firmly. "The inn will be a success. Whether it is or it isn't, though, that's none of your concern."

As if he hadn't listened to a word she'd said, Sam continued, "Look. I'll help you out. I'll send you a plane ticket. You can be here by the end of the week. And everything will go back to the way it was."

That was the problem. She didn't want to go back to the way things were.

"Save your breath, Sam. I am not flying to DC. Or coming back to you just because you snap your fingers and tell me that's what you want me to do. *You* walked out on our marriage. Not me. Now you've had a change of heart. Well, so have I. I'm building a new life here. I've made a commitment to Erin and Michelle and Nina, and I'm not walking away from it."

"You've got to be kidding." Sam's voice rose until Reggie had to hold the phone away from her ear. "I make one little mistake, and you're never going to forgive me?"

It had been more than one mistake, and he knew it. For the moment, she let his comment slide. It wouldn't do either of them any good if they got out a chalkboard and started listing who'd done what to whom. Sam would write, "No baby," and that would be the end of it. He'd always hold that against her.

"Forgiveness has nothing to do with it," she said, her voice low and even. "I'm just saying I'm not coming back."

"You little—" On the other end of the line, Sam took a breath. In his most lawyerly voice, he pleaded, "You've got to give us a second chance. My career is at stake here. I'll do whatever it takes. We can see a marriage counselor if that's what you want. I—I'll even spring for another round of IVF. You name it. You give up this foolish notion of going into business with your friends and whatever you want, it's yours."

Reggie's chest squeezed. She sucked in air. Did he mean it? Would he really foot the bill for more fertility treatments? Could she have a baby of her own after all? Tears sprang to her eyes. She shook her head as her dream of the future dissolved.

People said "distance makes the heart grow fonder." In her case, though, the thousand miles between them had given her a new perspective. Yes, she'd wanted a baby, wanted them to be a family. But more than just a baby, she'd wanted to raise their child in a loving home. Which was kind of impossible with Sam. She could see now that he was manipulative and demanding. That he put her down every chance he had. That wasn't an atmosphere she wanted to live in, much less raise a child in. She couldn't believe it had taken her this long to see the truth.

"No, Sam," she said simply. "It's over between us."

Saying the words lifted a tremendous weight from her shoulders. Sam didn't love her. He wanted to further his career; that's the only reason he wanted her back.

"If you have anything else to say to me, I suggest you get in touch with my attorney."

She clicked off. The phone rang again almost immediately. Her finger hovered over the Decline Call button. Noticing Nina's name on the screen, she answered instead.

"Dinner's almost ready. Fifteen minutes?"

"I'll be right in." Surprised her fingers didn't shake even a little, she returned the phone to her back pocket and headed for the house. She, Michelle, Erin and Nina usually discussed the day over dinner. She normally didn't have much to contribute, but she would tonight. Beginning with the old pickup truck which, thanks to Chris's help, was now roadworthy again. Speaking of Chris, Erin and Nina had seemed to like when they met earlier today. She was glad of that.

She sensed he'd make a good friend. He made her feel good about herself, something she was learning to appreciate after putting up with Sam's constant put-downs. Which brought her to the man himself and the fact that she'd stamped their marriage with a big, red "Over and Done."

She dusted her hands on her shorts and whistled on her way to the house and dinner with the three people she trusted the most in the world.

# Eleven

## Michelle

Michelle folded her hands on the table at Maggie's Diner. She took a deep breath and congratulated herself on making it through the practice run of her business plan. She hadn't stumbled over a single word. She looked across the table to Dave. The man's lips didn't turn up at the corners as they were prone to do, but she caught the glimmer of satisfaction in his eyes.

She'd nailed it.

It hadn't been easy. Dave hadn't been joking when he told her he'd help her make her business plan letter-perfect. In keeping with his promise, he'd called frequently to offer suggestions or comments. Why, his name had appeared on the screen of her cell phone a dozen times or more over the past week! Sometimes he pointed out items she might have otherwise left out of the proposal. Other times he asked questions that sent her madly scrambling for answers the town council would expect her to have at her fingertips. Once or twice, he called just to deliver much-appreciated encouragement.

Whatever his reason, though, he always made time to ask how her day was going, whether the house was beginning to feel like home yet, or if she'd taken a break to go for a walk on the beach that day. Not that he lingered. She often heard the trill of other phones or the squeak of his desk chair and knew he'd called between appointments. Occasionally he'd call her when he was on the road, the hum of his tires providing a background to their conversation.

She'd started to look forward to hearing from him and hoped they'd continue to stay in touch once the town council gave the inn the go-ahead. Speaking of which, she smiled sweetly at the man seated across the table and asked, "Any questions?"

Dave's brows knitted. "Just one."

Michelle tensed.

"Do you want a BLT for lunch or a turkey club?"

She let out the breath she hadn't realized

she'd been holding as the smile she'd been hoping for broke across Dave's face. Approval shone in his eyes.

"It's a good proposal?" she asked.

"It's a *great* proposal," Dave insisted. "The council would be foolish not to give you the green light. I think they'll especially like to hear that, since you're planning to maintain the house and the property pretty much as they are now, the inn will have very little impact on the environment. All those new houses Orson wanted to build would have put extra strain on the infrastructure. They'll love the bit about hiring local workers for the renovations and painting, too. That was another negative in Orson's plan—his backers wanted to bring in their own builders and contractors."

"We've already hired Chris Johnson to handle some of the repair work around the place." Reggie had suggested it at dinner last week. They'd identified a half dozen projects that didn't require them to pull permits—those bigger jobs were on hold until the council approved the zoning change—and put him to work. He'd begun repairs on the front porch the next day.

"Chris is one of the good guys. I have to give him a lot of credit for his commitment to raising that little girl of his." Dave sipped from his glass of iced tea. "You heard how he lost his wife," he murmured softly.

"Yes. Reggie filled us in. We all got to meet the little princess yesterday. Chris came over to measure for a new top railing. He brought Hope with him." She laughed. The job should have taken five minutes, but she, Erin and Nina had insisted on playing with the baby. She was sure Reggie would have joined in, but she was working around the lake out back. As it was, Chris had spent the better part of an hour at the house. "It was touching to see how devoted he is to her."

For half a second, she wondered how differently her own life would have turned out if Nancy Simmons had raised her instead of giving her up for adoption. Michelle sloughed the question aside. She'd had not just an okay life but a very good one. Her adoptive parents had doted on her. While they hadn't been rich by any means, she'd never known hunger except by choice. She'd grown up safe and warm and loved—who could ask for more than that? Not her.

She smiled at Dave. "Which do you recommend—the club or the BLT?"

Dave picked up the menu their waitress had left on the table. He ran a finger down the sandwich options. "I'm hankering for a BLT, but my doctor says I should have the club...without bacon." He shrugged. "Gotta watch that cholesterol, you know."

"I hear you." Her own numbers were right where they ought to be, but Allen's had been off the chart. When his had started inching toward the red zone, she'd cut down on the meat in their diet and centered more meals around fresh fruits and vegetables. She'd been puzzled when the change hadn't helped...until she discovered a half dozen empty fast-food bags in the back seat of her husband's car. Seeing how careful Dave was with his diet made her wonder if Allen might still be around if he'd paid attention to his doctor's orders.

Their waitress swung by the table. "Y'all ready to order? Can I get ya a refill on your drinks?"

Dave nodded. "Thanks for letting us hang out for a while, Sally." They'd been sitting in the back booth for nearly an hour while they fine-tuned Michelle's pitch to the town council.

"Oh, pshaw. T'weren't no problem. You caught us when it was slow. Startin' to fill up now, though." Sally tapped her order pad.

Taking the hint, Michelle looked up at her. "Your daily special is grouper. Is it fresh?"

"Right off the boat." Sally crossed her heart.

"Maggie's son caught 'em last night in the Gulf. We got the dinner portion with your choice of two sides. Or grilled on a bun."

The fish sounded good, and Michelle ordered a sandwich. Dave asked for a turkey club without bacon or mayo. Sally refilled their drinks and promised to be back soon with their orders. After she hurried off to the kitchen, Michelle surveyed the diner. The same four retirees she'd spotted on her last visit occupied one of the tables. She nodded to them.

Keeping her voice barely above a whisper, she observed, "They seem to spend a lot of time here."

"Maggie's is a second home for those boys," Dave said in the same low tone. "You're likely to find them here most any day of the week, 'cept Sundays. Where else can you sit all day in the air-conditioning, drinking tea and chewing the fat?"

"Maggie doesn't mind?"

"Oh, she does." Dave tipped his head toward the group. "But see the skinny guy in the plaid shirt? That's Maggie's Uncle Jack. Her mom would flat tan her hide if Maggie tossed him and his cronies out."

Laughter bubbled up from Michelle's midsection at the idea of the sixty-something restaurant owner getting in trouble with her mother. She pressed her napkin against her lips to smother her giggles. As she did, a new thought occurred to her. She tried it on for size.

"Maybe we could help out with that. The house has lots of room. Once the inn and the café are operational, we could set aside one of the parlors as a meeting place." She pictured a half dozen comfortable chairs in the library, a tall dispenser of sweet tea and plates of cookies on the sideboard.

"You do that, and Maggie will be forever in your debt." Dave nodded to himself.

"Well." Michelle blotted her lips. "Don't say anything to her about it right now. I have to run the idea past Erin, Nina and Reggie first. But I don't see why they'd object. Assuming the council approves our proposal, that is."

"You give your talk the same way you did today, and everything will turn out just fine." Dave reached for her hand.

His gentle squeeze was over in a blink, but Michelle appreciated it. Dave's light, reassuring touch was just what she needed. She would have told him so, but she spotted Sally on approach carrying a full tray. She moved her glass of iced tea to one side.

The waitress doled out their lunches, silverware wrapped in fresh napkins, and topped off their drink orders with the efficiency that came from long years of practice. Last of all, she set a bottle of tartar sauce at Michelle's elbow. "Anything else I can get you?" Sally asked. When there wasn't, she sped off toward a pair of newcomers who'd chosen the booth closest to the cash register.

Michelle eyed her sandwich. A full inch of thick, glossy grilled fish stuck out on either side of a lightly toasted bun. Enough lettuce and sliced tomato for a small salad were arrayed along one edge of her plate. A handful of potato chips took up the rest of the space. She inhaled a whiff of briny goodness.

"Oh, my stars," she said. "Maggie certainly doesn't skimp on portions. And this fish! It looks delicious."

"Looks like we both made good choices." Dave removed the toothpick from one quarter of his triple-decker sandwich. "Dig in." He took a bite.

As marvelous as the fish tasted, Michelle knew she'd never in a million years eat the entire thing in one sitting. She carefully cut her sandwich in half before taking her first bite. A bite she enjoyed very much. A nice blend of seasonings enhanced the flavor of the mild, white fish, while the crispy edges of the bun added a satisfying crunch. "Mmmmm," she said, not able to say anything more with her mouth full.

They chatted between bites. Dave's friendly manner encouraged her to confess how disappointed she'd been when Ashley and Aaron couldn't make it down for Mother's Day. "I thought maybe they'd surprise me with a quick visit, but no. The day passed without a knock on the door. I understand they're busy. I don't want to take them away from their studies..."

"But still," Dave said, completing her thought. He shook his head. "Raising young adults is tough. I ask myself all the time if I'm doing the right thing with Sarah. Right now, she needs a new car. She's driving the used one I bought her when she started law school. It has over a hundred thousand miles on it, and I worry that it might break down and strand her somewhere. I told her to save up for a new one, but she'd rather eat out and carry a designer handbag. I could just take her to the car dealership. But what would that teach her? That if she just waits long enough, Daddy will solve every problem?"

Michelle chewed slowly and swallowed. Their father had promised to give Aaron and Ashley new cars when they graduated. That she couldn't was another bone of contention between them. "I don't know about buying her a car—that's a decision only you can make. In the meantime, though, why don't you get her a Triple A membership?"

Dave stilled, his sandwich halfway to his mouth. "Brilliant idea," he said. He whipped out his phone, and his thumbs flew across the keys. "I'm sending myself a reminder to do exactly that." Finished, he looked up. His eyes sought hers. "Thank you. You've given me such peace of mind."

Michelle felt her cheeks warm. She hadn't really done anything to deserve Dave's thanks. Advising another parent on how to handle their child was easy. Handling your own kids, that was the tough part.

The conversation drifted from subject to subject while they finished their lunches. They each swapped a story or two about their childhoods. Michelle made a note to remind Reggie to be wary of snakes when Dave spoke of finding a nest of baby water moccasins while exploring the woods behind his house as a young teen. She laughed at the pranks he and his friends had pulled on some of his neighbors. Far too soon, though, he slid his plate to one side.

"I hate to leave, but I need to get back to the office," he said with obvious reluctance.

"Oh, my goodness. I have to go, too. The rest of the crew will be wondering where I've gotten off to." Instead of dinner tonight, Nina was preparing hors d'oeuvres and sweet treats. They were going to sample them and choose the best ones for the open house. Michelle gathered up her papers and the takeout box that held the rest of her sandwich. When she dug in her purse for her wallet, Dave insisted on paying for their lunch.

"Okay," she said brightly. "But next time, it's my treat."

"I think next time might be the open house. I'll see you Saturday?"

"I can't believe it's gotten here so quickly," Michelle said as they headed across a parking lot of crushed shells a few minutes later. Heat and humidity pressed down on her like a wet blanket, and she prayed for a break in the weather before the weekend. She and her friends had worked like demons cleaning and scrubbing, vacuuming and polishing. And there was more to do. Other than their own rooms, they hadn't begun to tackle the upstairs yet.

"Was the open house your idea?" Dave asked as they stepped into the shade of the big oak in the middle of the lot.

"No, that was Reggie's." Her young friend was surprisingly savvy about marketing.

"Be sure to tell her it was a good idea. Everyone I've spoken to in town is excited about it. This could go a long way toward convincing the council to vote in your favor." At the bumper of her car, he gave a cheery wave goodbye and stepped smartly to his own vehicle.

Pleased with how the morning had gone, Michelle drove back to the house with a smile on her face. She had to admit, she'd enjoyed Dave's company. She had a feeling they'd be good friends. Not that she'd ever think of him as more than that. She'd had the one great love in her life. She wasn't going to tempt fate a second time. But she wouldn't turn down the occasional invitation to lunch or a movie. That's what friends did with one another, wasn't it?

# Twelve

## *Reggie*

**B**eyond the gate, heat shimmered off the blacktop. Reggie propped one arm atop the handle of her spade. She surveyed her work while she mopped sweat from her brow. Evenly spaced hostas formed straight lines on either side of the freshly graveled driveway. Behind them, the long stalks of bird of paradise raised their purple and orange heads above wide, waxy leaves. Firecracker and chenille plants filled the gaps between the other bushes. With nary a weed in sight, vibrant colors and healthy plants welcomed new arrivals onto the property.

Happy with her work, she wrenched the shovel from the ground. With the tool on her shoulder, she strode toward the beat-up truck Chris had helped her get working again. She placed the spade in the pickup's bed. As she did, she quickly reviewed the list of chores she still had to finish before the open house. Other than a few last-minute tasks—like sweeping off the walkways and the porch—only one big item remained. She needed to weed the flower beds closest to the house.

She'd been putting off that particular task ever since Chris had started replacing the broken slats and the wooden railing. She'd sort of been avoiding him. The last few weeks, spending her days doing the kind of work she loved and hanging out with her sister and her friends at night, she hadn't exactly been able to forget how much she'd wanted a baby or that her inability to get pregnant had destroyed her marriage. But her shattered dreams had faded a bit until they no longer occupied her every waking moment.

But that day, the one when Chris showed up with Hope on his hip? Yeah, that day, one glimpse of the baby's apple cheeks had melted her insides. So much longing for what she was never going to have had washed over her that she'd thought she might drown in it. Struggling to stay afloat, she'd rushed out the back door, grabbed an armload of tools and headed for the lake. It was as far away from Chris and his daughter as she could get. She'd spent the entire day taking her frustrations out on the poor, hapless plants that had grown too close to the water's edge.

And it had helped.

By the time she'd cleared the shoreline and stood, exhausted, looking out over the water, she'd stopped feeling sorry for herself. Which lasted until she realized that, in her rush to get away from Chris and his daughter, she hadn't stopped to put on sunblock. Her arms and legs had turned a bright, cherry red that stung for days.

She hadn't spoken to Chris since. But she couldn't avoid him any longer. Not if she was going to get those flower beds weeded before the weekend. She took a long, slow breath. She didn't have any choice. She'd have to talk to the man. Preferably without melting into a puddle of hormones.

After climbing into the truck, she checked her phone for messages. The number three glowed above a tiny icon. Three missed calls, all from Sheldon Cole, the divorce attorney Erin had hired for her. She thumbed to the message center. The lawyer had left two voice mails. Her lips tightened. After her last conversation with Sam, she'd left word for the attorney to move forward with the separation agreement at his earliest convenience. Had he hit a snag? She pressed play.

*"Ms. Frank, please call the office as soon as possible."*

Now what?

Reggie removed her hat and set it on the seat beside her. Her hair tumbled loose around her shoulders. She ran her fingers through the damp strands while she listened to the second message, which provided no more information than the first. Grabbing a scrunchie that hung from the rear-view mirror, she smoothed her hair into a ponytail and secured it in place. She took a breath and punched the number for the attorney's office.

A receptionist answered on the second ring. Expecting to be put on hold for a while, Reggie was surprised when the woman put her call through almost immediately.

"Ms. Frank, thanks so much for getting back to me." Mr. Cole's voice was as smooth and elegant as a rose petal. "I'm afraid I've run into a problem with your filing."

"Oh?" Reggie's stomach clenched. What had Sam done now?

"Yes. I'm sure I made it clear in our first conversation that, according to Virginia law, you and your husband cannot live together for a period of six months prior to the divorce."

Reggie's brows knitted. So far, so good. Sam lived and worked in Virginia. She no longer did. "Yes. We've been over that."

"Or have, um, marital relations?"

"Right. That was my understanding." Where on earth was he going with this?

"Ms. Frank, there's no easy way to ask this, so I'm going to be quite blunt. In going over your husband's financials, we discovered he has a standing reservation at the Hyatt Regency Capitol Hill on alternate Thursday afternoons. On each of those days, he and a guest have lunch downstairs at Article One, a rather tony restaurant. Then, I assume they adjourn to the suite."

Reggie froze. Her breath seized in her chest when the lawyer stopped talking. She heard the soft chink of ice cubes in a glass, followed by a quiet thunk. A thin, white bird landed on the hood of the truck. It stood there, preening its feathers as if this were an ordinary day.

"Ms. Frank, are you there?" her attorney asked at length.

She cleared her throat. "Yes," she croaked.

"Good. Please think very carefully about the answer to the question I'm about to ask, Ms. Frank. Have you been meeting your husband on those Thursday afternoons? Because if you are, I'm concerned the judge will look at the time you and Mr. Frank are spending together and rule you are not, in fact, fulfilling that separation requirement. On the other hand, if you're not, well, that might change how we proceed."

Reggie's mouth worked, but nothing came out. She swallowed and tried again. "At the Hyatt?"

"Yes."

"In the District?"

"Yes."

"How long?"

"Pardon?" The question must have caught the attorney off guard.

"How long has this been going on?" she asked. The bird finished doing whatever birds did and flew off. "How long has Sam had this reservation?"

"Well, I—" Papers rustled. "Three years, give or take a month or two."

"I take it things haven't changed in the last few weeks?" Her stomach quivered. She took a breath. "You do know I moved to Florida last month, don't you?"

More paper shuffled. "Yes. I believe I have that in my notes."

"It's true. It's also true that I haven't been

back to Virginia—or the District—in four weeks. And I've never, ever, met my husband for lunch—or anything else—at the Hyatt Regency. Whoever Sam is entertaining in that suite every other week, it's not me. It never has been."

"Oh. I see." On the other end of the line, a pen made scratching noises. "Well, that certainly, um, changes things."

Suddenly, she felt as if a great weight had been lifted off her shoulders. All this time she'd blamed the end of their marriage on her inability to get pregnant. But Sam hadn't walked out on her because she couldn't give him a child. He'd been unfaithful. He'd found someone else. That's why he'd left her. She ran her tongue over her lips to moisten them. Now, more than ever, she wanted things over between Sam and her. "How does this impact the separation and divorce?"

"That depends." The attorney, whose voice had wobbled for just a second there, resumed his polished delivery. "It could have no effect at all if you want to proceed as we'd planned. We'd simply set this information aside, wait the required six months, and the rest is fairly automatic. On the other hand, you could choose to pursue a fault-based divorce. In this case, the fault would be adultery. That type of dissolution can be finalized much faster. However, there's a catch."

There's always a catch, she thought. "What is it?"

"The hotel reservation and receipts for meals aren't enough. The State of Virginia requires a witness to the, um, deed itself. I can hire someone, if you like. We work with a reputable private investigator."

But she was already shaking her head. Sam might have broken their wedding vows, but she wouldn't stoop so low as to hire someone to spy on him. Or—her stomach performed an ungainly tuck and roll—take pictures. "That won't be necessary. Let's stick with the original plan. Have you filed the separation agreement yet?"

"We're all set on our end. Mr. Frank has been dragging his heels, though. He hasn't signed his copy."

Though she knew the answer without asking, she asked, "He's still acting as his own attorney?"

"Yes. I believe he is." A hint of disdain crept into her lawyer's tone.

*Of course he was.* Her soon-to-be-ex was too proud of his own skills to let someone else handle his case.

"Let Sam know we know about the Hyatt. I'm pretty sure that'll get things moving in the right direction." She'd bet her last dollar the instant Sam understood she knew how he'd been spending his Thursday afternoons, he'd sign the papers. He wouldn't risk having his affair whispered about in the hallowed halls of Shorter and Grominsky. Despite Sam's insistence that a divorce would ruin his chances for a big promotion, she had no doubt Mr. Grominsky would overlook it…as long as Sam didn't shoulder the blame. But if word leaked that he'd been unfaithful, it would kill any hope he had of ever making partner.

"Yes, ma'am. I'll make that call today. And Ms. Frank?"

"Yes?"

"You've certainly taken this well. I've had other clients who, well, let's say it wasn't their best moment." Admiration colored the attorney's words. "Still, I'm sorry. No divorce is easy, but…"

"Don't worry about it, Mr. Cole. I think on some level I've suspected the truth for quite some time. I just didn't want to believe it."

After the conversation ended, she leaned against the headrest. She hadn't lied to save face in front of a man she'd never met. All those Thursdays when Sam had come home late looking like something the cat had dragged in. The occasional whiff of perfume she'd caught when she did their laundry. His secrecy about their bank accounts. The late-night phone calls he'd insisted on taking in another room…with the door closed. How, claiming it was a work thing, he'd never given her his email password.

So many secrets. Too many secrets.

The warning signs had been right in front of her. But she'd been so focused on making a family, she'd refused to see them. Had she been trying, even then, to save her marriage by having a baby?

She had.

She took a minute to let the truth sink in. Yes, she still wanted a baby, and it still hurt that she couldn't have one. But the constant, driving *need* to get pregnant, to give birth, had evaporated. The same way the morning dew disappeared when the sun warmed the grass and leaves. She felt lighter somehow. More content with herself.

She started the truck and put it in gear. She had work to do, a few finishing touches to put on her special project behind the gardener's shed and some flower beds to weed. If the latter meant being around Chris, she was okay with that. In fact, she was sort of looking forward to seeing him—and his daughter—at the open house this weekend.

# Thirteen

## Reggie

*R*eggie felt like she was waking after a long, long nap. She showered, washed her hair and gave the long ends an extra dose of conditioner. She rubbed lotion into her elbows, her shoulders, her neck. Searching in her closet, she unearthed a sundress she hadn't worn since her arrival in Florida. It was perfect for a spring evening when the weather had turned hot and sticky. She stepped into it. Crossing to the dresser, she pulled open the small drawer where she kept her makeup. Fixing her face in the tall mirror didn't require much work. Just a little powder to tone down the shine. A bit of mascara. A slash of nude pink lipstick.

She flexed her fingers. Fearing she'd lose the two-carat diamond while she was digging in the dirt somewhere, she'd stashed her engagement ring in the bottom of her jewelry box, only slipping it over her knuckle on special occasions. But the matching gold band she wore glinted in the light from the lamp on her dresser.

*It was time.*

She tugged the ring from the third finger of her left hand. Eyeing the thin white line it left behind, she applied a dab more lotion to her fingers. No doubt the color would fill in soon enough.

She checked her image in the mirror. Reddish-gold strands of hair curled softly around her shoulders. The dark mascara framed her blue eyes. The light lipstick made her lips look plumper. Her arms and shoulders had bronzed under the Florida sun, giving them a subtle, healthy glow.

She smiled at the total effect, which was far different from the slightly unkempt look she'd sported in recent weeks.

She might as well admit it. Ever since Sam had called it quits on their marriage, she'd been going through the motions while blame hung like an albatross around her neck.

But no more.

Finding out about Sam's affair, or affairs—had there been more than one?—had freed her.

She felt buoyant. Like a helium balloon that had broken free of its tether. She sniffed the air. Whatever Nina was cooking in the kitchen, it smelled good. Her stomach rumbled a faint reminder that she was actually hungry for the first time in a good, long while. Humming happily, she headed down to dinner.

"Someone looks nice tonight. Hot date?" Sipping from a tall, narrow glass, Michelle leaned against the kitchen counter.

"Dinner with three of my best friends. Does that count?" Reggie scanned the room. Nina stood by the mammoth Aga oven, one hand on the door handle, the other encased in a thick mitt while she waited for the timer on her phone to sound. At the refrigerator, Erin lifted a tray from the middle shelf. Tiny morsels of something that looked like the deconstructed flag of Italy dotted the dish.

"Thought you might be meeting Chris for a drink or something." Nina looked away from her phone long enough to give her eyebrows a suggestive waggle. "From the way you two were joking around out there today, I thought maybe you had something going on."

Reggie's smile deepened at the memory of the hours she'd spent weeding the flower beds while Chris tore out a section of the porch railing.

"We did have fun this afternoon. It helps to have someone to talk to. Makes the work go so much faster."

She'd half-expected a few tense minutes after she stepped from the old pickup truck earlier, but she needn't have worried. Whether Chris had noticed her disappearing act the last few days or not, he didn't say. Instead, he'd given her that lopsided smile that made her feel all warm and happy inside. They'd quickly slipped right back into an easy give-and-take. But she needed to set the record straight with her sister and her friends—she didn't want them to get the wrong idea about her and Chris.

"So there's nothing going on between you?" Nina persisted.

"What with Hope and losing his wife and all, Chris is dealing with enough right now. The last thing he needs right now is to get involved with someone. But I get the impression he could use a friend. That's what I'm trying to be. His friend." She lifted one shoulder. "Even if I were interested in him as something more than that, it's not gonna happen. I've declared all men off-limits, at least till my divorce is final. Probably a whole lot longer than that."

Reggie paused. *Should she tell them?* She had to. She'd vowed not to keep any more secrets.

"But it *is* time to move on." Pointing to the white reminder of her wedding band, she lifted her left hand.

"Reggie! You took off your ring?" Erin let out a high-pitched squeal. "Eeeeee! That's a big step!"

"Huge!" chimed Michelle. She twisted the bands on her own hand.

"What brought this on?" Nina asked. The cook opened the oven door and peered inside.

"I'll tell you. But first, I think we all need a drink. Mind if I crack open a bottle of merlot?"

"You can, but Nina made punch." Erin lifted a glass filled with an orangey concoction. "We're thinking of making it the inn's signature drink. Want some?"

"Do beggar's lice stick to socks?"

"Ugh, don't remind me," Erin protested. She poured a small amount from a tall pitcher. "I picked some up when I was scoping out a spot to launch the kayak. Took forever to pick them off my shorts."

"Shorts, nothing." Reggie laughed. The hard-to-eradicate weed produced an abundance of small brown seeds that stuck like glue to almost anything that brushed against them. Try as she might to get them all off her socks at the end of the day, she invariably missed one or two. Which led to all sorts of problems. The pesky seeds had a nasty habit of migrating from socks to *something else* in the washing machine. "The panties I pulled from my drawer this morning had one stuck in what could have been a very uncomfortable spot."

While the others laughed, she took the glass Erin handed her. She sipped. The taste of peach mingled with mint and rum swirled across her tongue.

"Our signature drink, you said?" She pretended to frown.

"Why? You don't like it?" A tiny divot appeared between Nina's brows.

"I like it a lot," she declared. She tossed back the rest of the sample and held her glass out for more. "Maybe too much. We should name it."

"Sugar Sand Punch," Michelle called while Erin filled Reggie's glass.

"Hmm, no. Sorry, but 'sand' doesn't work," Nina objected.

Reggie swirled the mixture in her glass. The orange tones reminded her of the colors of the sunset. "What about Peach Sunset?" she asked.

"Maybe Gulf Coast Sunset?" Nina suggested.

"Even better." Reggie nodded.

The others chimed in agreeably, and the matter was settled.

Nina's cell phone dinged. In swift, graceful

motions, she pulled two trays from the oven and set them atop trivets. Grabbing a small grater and a block of Parmesan, she dusted one pan with cheese. The other, she sprinkled with the barest pinch of reddish powder. She stepped back, her hands on her hips. "Okay," she announced. "I think we're ready. Erin, get the other trays from the fridge, will you?"

While Erin complied, Nina took two more cookie sheets from the warming oven. Soon, various dishes—some hot, some cold—filled one end of the long counter. Nina clasped her hands below her waist. Her voice low and professional, she began her presentation.

"I've prepared eight different appetizers for you to sample this evening. It's my hope we can choose four of them to serve at the open house this weekend." Starting with the cold dishes, she pointed. "Here, we have honeydew melon cubes topped with feta and adorned with alfalfa sprout and black olive. Next are fruit skewers glazed with a honey cardamom reduction. Over there is a takeoff on avocado toast—this one features spicy guacamole on house-made melba rounds, garnished with sprigs of white radish. And last, the cherry tomatoes in this take on caprese salad have been injected with my own balsamic vinaigrette reduction. Any questions?"

"I have one," Reggie said. She shifted her weight from one foot to the other. "When can we eat?"

"Patience, little one," Nina said with a smile. "Now, the hot options include crispy sweet potato slices baked with a cream cheese and cranberry topping, dusted with a touch of ghost chili pepper." She pointed to another scrumptious-looking dish. "That's a Gulf Coast version of rumaki, using bacon-wrapped shrimp and water chestnuts. Next, we have a seared scallop topped with caviar and crème fraiche served on a painted clam shell. Aren't those adorable?" Without waiting for an answer, she continued in a fake Italian accent. "Meat-a-balls dusted with Parmesan. Mwah!" She kissed her fingers. "In this case, I used Florida bison rather than the traditional beef and pork mixture." She smoothed her hands over her apron. "Oh, and there's one more." Rushing to the warming oven, she returned bearing a tray of grilled sausage slices on tooth-picks. "We can't forget Gus's sausages."

"Bravo, Chef Nina. You've outdone yourself." Reggie clapped her hands, and the others joined in.

"I'm intrigued by some of these. I can already tell we're going to have a very tough time narrowing our choices," said Michelle once the room quieted. She took a square, white plate from the stack at the end of the counter and began filling it with one or two bites of each dish.

"No need to vote on the sausage. We're definitely serving that," Nina said, arranging the tray on the counter. "I've already placed an order with Gus for Thursday. Wherever possible, I've chosen local products. The shrimp and scallops came from a seafood market just down the coast a bit—everything there is fresh-caught. The farmers' market in town carries a pretty good selection of produce. We'll buy from them until our own garden is ready for harvest."

"Speaking of...all the fruits and veggies are up and looking good. We should have our first crop of beans and tomatoes by mid-July." Reggie snagged a toothpick and popped one of the sausage slices into her mouth. "Mmmmm," she moaned as she chewed. "Best ev-eh."

With some good-natured jostling, Erin, Reggie and Nina fell in line behind Michelle. Soon the many options crowded everyone's plates. The women gathered at the kitchen table, where Nina had left printed menus, along with a pencil, at each of their places.

"Be sure to rank each item, one through eight. We'll tally up the scores to determine the winners," the chef said as she slipped into the last spot at the table.

Just as Michelle had predicted, whittling down the options was tough. While every dish was mouthwateringly good, each of them had their favorites. Erin couldn't get enough of the meatballs. Michelle nearly waxed poetic over the seared scallops in their pretty shells, while Reggie loved all the veggie dishes. They nearly came to mock blows until Nina reminded them that the open house was just the first of many parties at the inn. That made it easier for Reggie to agree when the guacamole toast and the sweet potato slices she dearly loved were stricken from the menu. When they finished, Nina brought out a carafe of coffee and a plate of cookies.

"We've ordered a cake from the bakery in Sugar Sand Beach for Saturday night," Michelle said. She dunked her cookie into her coffee cup.

"The gift baskets we delivered were such a hit with all the business owners in town that we'll serve our own fresh-baked cookies, as well," Erin explained while Nina nodded in agreement.

Reggie patted her full tummy. She leaned back in her chair, feeling more content than she had in a long time.

Erin leaned toward her. "Did you just decide it was time to remove your ring? Or is there something you want to share with us?"

"Yeah. About that." Reggie nodded. "It's quite the story. I was talking with my attorney earlier today. Mr. Cole asked if Sam and I had been fooling around at some swanky hotel down in the District when we were supposed to be separated. He said that wouldn't play well with the judge when it came time to finalize our divorce."

Expecting a chorus of shocked gasps and protests, Reggie leaned back in her chair when no one made a sound. Her brows knitted, and she scanned the faces at the table. Sympathy softened her friends' expressions, but their eyes held a look she hadn't anticipated.

*Had they known?*

"It took us a while, but we figured out Sam's been having an affair, or a series of affairs, for going on three years now." Her gaze traveled from face to face. "But I guess you already knew that?"

Erin spoke first. "Not for sure. But we suspected."

"You're too good a person for Sam to walk out on you the way he did without a reason. Sadly, another woman is the usual reason," Michelle said without meeting Reggie's eyes.

"Almost always," Nina added. "We didn't say anything in case we were wrong. Please, don't be mad with us. We're sorry, so sorry this happened to you."

Reggie nodded. If her sister and her friends had had proof of Sam's involvement with someone else, they'd have told her. Of that, she had no doubt. It was time to put their minds at ease.

"Don't be. Sorry for me, that is." Reggie held her hands out, her palms open. "I'm relieved, actually. Finding out he's been unfaithful all this time takes a huge burden off me. See, ever since that night when Sam packed his bags and left, I've been blaming myself. All this time, I thought it was my fault our marriage failed."

Always ready to spring to her defense, Erin protested, "Why would you think that? You didn't do anything wrong!"

"There's something you don't know. I should have told you a long time ago." She took Erin's hand to soften the blow. "Sam and I, we've been trying to get pregnant for a couple of years now. We tried everything, including several rounds of IVF. That's why our credit cards were maxed out, why Sam thought I should pay those off myself. The night he called it quits, that was the same night I learned the latest IVF cycle had failed. Again. I was certain he left because I couldn't give him the son he's always wanted.

Turns out, it wasn't my fault at all. He left because...well, he's Sam."

"He's a jerk," declared Nina.

Erin started to put in her own two cents. "An as—"

"Stop!" Reggie threw up her hands. "I know, I know. I've called him a few names myself. But that's not who I want to be. I don't want to be one of those women who, ten years from now, goes out on a first date and can't stop talking about all the ways her ex betrayed her. I just want to get this divorce over with so I can move on with my life."

"Amen to that," Michelle said softly. "Remember Frannie Dumont?" The bottle blonde lived in Michelle's neighborhood and bent the ear of anyone who'd listen with endless stories about her evil ex-husband. They'd all been rather relieved when the woman stopped showing up at every gathering.

"Whatever happened to her?" Nina asked.

"She moved out West. Arizona, I think. In her Christmas card last year, she said something about how she'd had to sell her house because her ex..." Michelle left the rest hanging.

"She didn't!" Erin gave her head a sad shake.

"That's exactly what I don't want to have happen to me," Reggie said. "We're all going to take a few lumps in this life. We can let them make us bitter or better."

Nina nodded. "We can wallow in our problems or we can learn from them and move on."

Erin slung an arm around her shoulders. "Ah, Reggie. You don't have to worry about turning into a Frannie. But I am sorry this happened to you. We all are."

"Yes," Michelle said, her voice firm.

"I still might punch Sam's lights out next time I see him."

Reggie would have glared at Nina, but the brunette's saucy smile said she was only teasing.

Erin sat back. "Look, I know we have a lot to do between now and the open house on Saturday, but the first chance we get, I'm going to get you out on the water. There's nothing like the slap of the waves, the birds turning cartwheels overhead, the wind in your face to soothe your soul. You deserve it after all you've been through."

Despite reassuring everyone else that she was fine, Reggie felt tears sting the corners of her eyes. "Thanks," she said simply. "I'd like that."

# Fourteen

## Reggie

The morning of the open house dawned clear and breezy, a pleasant change from the sweltering heat that had held the Gulf coast in a tight fist for the past week. More accustomed to Virginia's mild spring, where Mother Nature's idea of a practical joke might be snow on April 1, Reggie, Michelle and Nina had been on edge the last few days. Even Erin, who usually thrived when the thermometer climbed above 90, had had a few irritable moments. But a passing front had moved through the area the day before. The cooling rain had ushered in a much-welcome break from the heat.

The change filled everyone in the house with fresh energy. Up before dawn, they all grabbed coffee and granola bars and got to work. Michelle prowled the downstairs rooms with a dust rag in one hand, a damp mop in the other. She stopped dusting only long enough to plump every pillow and straighten every cushion. Erin tackled the nearly spotless windows with a bottle of cleaner and a roll of paper towels before running a vacuum over the rugs. In a crisp, white apron, her hair pulled into a sleek ponytail, Nina stood at the kitchen counter before an immense bowl of ground bison seasoned with her own special recipe. One by one, she rolled hundreds of tiny meatballs. While she worked, she monitored several pots on the stove. Tantalizing smells filled the kitchen and drifted through the rest of the house.

Reggie murmured a good morning to the others as she fixed her coffee in a to-go cup. Heading outside before the morning dew dried, she gave her special project a final look. After that she cut armloads of flowers, which she arranged in tall vases on a bench she'd set up in the gardener's shed. She left the floral arrangements on the sun porch. From there, Michelle and Erin had agreed to distribute the vases throughout the downstairs.

Next she made the rounds outdoors, making sure no errant weeds had sprung up in the flower beds overnight, no critters had suddenly decided to dig a huge swimming hole in the front yard. She chuckled at that last one but then recalled Chris telling her about a pack of feral hogs that had unearthed every square inch of sod in front of the community center one year. She gave the lawn a second look and breathed a sigh of relief when she didn't spot a single snout-shaped hole.

After raking the graveled parking pad, she grabbed the piece of driftwood she'd turned into a Welcome sign and headed for the front gate. Making sure the sign hung level took a bit longer than she'd anticipated. By the time she finished, it was time for lunch.

At the house, she reviewed her list of things to do while she devoured a ham on rye she'd made up the night before. The garage, which hadn't received the same tender loving care as the house and grounds, had been locked up tight. She'd parked her truck nearby, leaving the wide graveled parking area available for guests. Before she went in to shower and dress, she'd sweep the porch and sidewalks one final time. She tapped her finger on the patch of bare skin between her knee and the hem of her shorts. There was only one thing left on her list and, smiling, she brushed a few crumbs from her fingers before she ducked inside.

"Have you seen Michelle?" she asked at the entrance to the kitchen. Though she'd carefully stomped her feet and wiped her boots on the doormat a dozen times, she didn't dare step foot into the chef's domain. At one end of the counter, Erin artfully arranged tiny alfalfa sprouts and slivers of black olives atop precisely cut cubes of honeydew. At the other, Nina looked up from an array of bowls filled with fruit. Threading a large strawberry on a wooden skewer, she nodded. "You just missed her. She left to pick up the cake from the bakery in town. Did you need something?"

Reggie shook her head. "No." If she did, she'd get it herself rather than throw the chef off schedule mere hours before an important event. And, as events went, today's open house rated somewhere near the top of the list in importance. "I have something to show her. Something I think she'll like." She scanned the kitchen. Nina and Erin worked at a steady pace. "How's it going in here?"

This time Erin raised her head. "Great, actually. We're ahead of schedule."

"Oh? You think you could take five minutes and join us on the front porch when Michelle gets back? It won't take longer than that. I promise."

Things like this were always more fun when all four of them were together.

"Unless something goes seriously wrong before then, I don't see why not." Nina added two plump blackberries to the skewer and topped it with a trio of the biggest blueberries Reggie had ever seen.

"Great. I'll holler when everything's ready." Checking the floor for boot prints and glad when she didn't spot any, Reggie backed out of the house. Outside once more, she sped across the backyard to the toolshed and grabbed a hand cart. She wheeled it around to the rear of the building where her secret gift for Michelle waited in the two large decorative pots she'd purchased at the Sugar Sand Beach Hardware store. After carefully loading the potted plants onto the cart, she very slowly trundled her precious cargo around to the front of the house. The pots were heavy, but she wrestled them up the porch steps one at a time. After arranging them on either side of the door, she stepped back, her arms folded. She frowned. Something about the placement wasn't exactly right. Bending, she scooted the pots another six inches apart. This time when she eyed the entryway, she smiled.

Moving quicker now that she didn't have to worry about the tall plants tipping over, she returned the hand truck to the toolshed. She locked up before trotting to the front of the house and up the steps. She'd just made it into position when she spotted Michelle's SUV turning off the main road onto the drive.

"Whew!" Reggie wiped imaginary sweat from her brow. She'd literally finished in the nick of time. She opened the front door and poked her head inside. "Nina. Erin. Can you come out here for a minute?"

"Coming!" one of them called, followed by the patter of feet hurrying down the hallway.

"Stand here." Reggie positioned Nina in front of one of the plants. The long apron the chef wore hid the pot from view.

"Wait a second." Erin bent low over a stem loaded with buds. "Are these what I think they are?" She pressed her fingers to her mouth.

"Really?" Nina spun around to face the plant. "Oh! Chelle will be so…"

"Shhh!" warned Reggie. "You'll spoil the surprise." She glanced over her shoulder just as Michelle's car crested the small hill. "Quick, Nina. Turn back around. Erin—"

"Got it." Following Nina's example, Erin stepped in front of the other plant.

Michelle's SUV rolled to a stop at the base of the steps. "What's all this?" she asked, emerging from the car a few seconds later. "I didn't expect a welcome party. Nothing's wrong, is it?"

A sudden nervous tension rushed through Reggie. What if Michelle didn't like her surprise? She'd spent weeks babying the plants, shopped for hours at the Sugar Sand Hardware Store until she found the perfect containers, dipped into her meager savings for fertilizer and the right kind of soil. But if Michelle didn't…

"Go ahead. Don't keep her waiting," Nina prompted.

*Might as well. It's too late to back out now.*

Reggie cleared her throat. "I—" She tossed a sidelong glance to Erin, who shook her head no. "We," she corrected, deciding it was only right to include the others. "We wanted to give you a special gift to celebrate the first open house at our new home. We've all worked hard to get the house in shape for today, but no one has done more than you. And, as our way of saying thanks for dragging us along into this new, exciting chapter in our lives, we hope you'll like these."

Without being told, Erin and Nina stepped away from the door to give Michelle her first glimpse of oval leaves with uniformly jagged edges that crowded long, thorny canes. Dozens of tiny buds sprouted from smaller branches.

"I was hoping for one or two flowers, but I guess it's a little early yet," Reggie apologized. Actually, she'd thanked her lucky stars more than once that the plants had even survived the trip. It was an absolute miracle they'd formed buds at all.

"Well, that's so nice of you girls, but really, you didn't have to." Michelle started up the stairs. Her foot on the top step, she stopped. She blinked several times in rapid succession. "Wait." She shook her head, then looked closer. "Are those...? They look an awful lot like...Are those *Allen's* roses?" Her voice trembled. Her eyes wide, she stared first at Reggie before glancing at Erin and Nina.

Reggie nodded. "I asked the new owners if they'd mind if we took a couple of the rose bushes for your new house. They were very sweet about it. I've been showering these babies with TLC ever since we left Fairfax."

Erin slipped one arm around Reggie's waist. "This was all Reggie's idea, Chelle. Though she said we'd helped, Nina and I didn't know a thing about it until just before you arrived."

"Oh!" Tears welled in Michelle's eyes. "This is..." She swiped at her cheeks. After crossing the porch in three quick strides, she bent to rub one of the leaves between her fingers. Her mouth gaped open. "I can't believe it. This is one of the nicest things anyone's ever done for me." Straightening, she wrapped Reggie in a tight embrace. "I can't thank you enough," she whispered. Michelle's head lifted. Her gaze traveled from one face to another before dropping once more to the plants. "With the four of us here, and now the rose bushes, this place finally feels like home."

Erin patted Michelle's back while Nina stepped closer. Soon, all four of them were locked in a group hug. By the time they stepped apart, four pairs of eyes sparkled with tears.

Nina clapped her hands. "Look, I hate to break this up, but I still have a ton of work to do and only"—she checked her watch—"four hours to do it in."

"I'm headed up to shower and change, but I'll help out as soon as I can," Reggie said.

"I need to get the cake out of the car and set it up in the kitchen." Michelle wiped her eyes and focused on Nina. "We're still serving food buffet-style from the counters, right?"

"Right," answered Erin as Nina darted back inside. "Let's get to work, people. Time's a-wasting."

# Fifteen

## Reggie

Note to self," Reggie murmured, holding the potted philodendron at arm's length. The plant had been over-watered. Liquid threatened to spill over the rim onto the handkerchief-print T-shirt dress she'd worn for the party. "The next time we invite the neighborhood in for a visit, hire a plant-carrier."

Starting a half hour before the appointed time, cars had begun turning in at the Welcome sign she'd hung on the gate. Within minutes, guests—some in beachwear, others dressed to the nines—had piled out of cars, trucks and even two golf carts. No matter what their mode of transportation or their clothing choice, they all had one thing in common—not a single party had arrived empty-handed. Soon, casseroles and pound cakes covered every spare inch of counter space in the kitchen, and the house smelled like a floral shop.

Giving up on finding an empty table in the library, Reggie set the plant—a gift from Cathy at Beach Cuts & Curls—on a bookshelf and hurriedly retraced her steps. On her way back to the door where Michelle was still greeting new arrivals, she spotted Erin in the front parlor. Her sister had worn a steel-gray hanbok she'd bought on one of her trips to Taiwan. Instead of the country's more traditional blousy skirt, she'd tucked the top with its signature crisscrossed closure into a pair of high-waisted white palazzo pants. The outfit was a conversation starter and, looking cool and elegant, Erin stood in the center of a group of guests. Entertaining them with stories of her travels, Reggie thought and smiled. She lingered in the hallway until she caught her sister's surreptitious nod. Reassured that everything was going well, she moved on.

She thought about taking a quick detour through the kitchen, but she'd peeked in on Nina fifteen minutes earlier. Dressed in chef's whites, her shiny dark hair pulled into a sleek bun, Nina had looked perfectly at ease as she divided her time between refilling the serving dishes and making friends.

Reggie laughed softly. The deluge of casserole dishes and desserts must have been a shock. Nevertheless, Nina had taken it in stride. Murmuring her thanks, she'd sliced the first few pound cakes and deftly arranged the pieces on a spare serving tray. She'd stashed the later arrivals in the pantry. As for the casseroles, anything hot and ready to serve went on a spare table, while those that required heating had gone straight into the fridge or freezer.

How had the cook handled guests who asked why their particular dish hadn't been served, Reggie wondered. She shook her head. She needn't worry. Nina was sure to have a ready answer and a sweet smile to go with it.

Approaching the front door, Reggie spied the house's official owner greeting their latest arrival. She whistled with admiration for her friend. Though she'd been on her feet for well over two hours, Michelle's smile hadn't wilted in the slightest. The short-sleeve sheath dress she'd worn to their first meeting with Dave Rollins looked as crisp and clean as it had when Michelle walked down the stairs just before the first guest rang the doorbell.

Wearing her own wide smile, Reggie stepped to her friend's side while Michelle chatted with a tall man who'd paired a crisp polo shirt with tan slacks and boat shoes. After the two exchanged the usual pleasantries, Michelle peered up at the new arrival. "Dr. Stewart, this is my very good friend Reggie Frank. Dr. Stewart runs the veterinary clinic in town," she said by way of introduction.

"I'm sure Nina will be glad to hear there's a veterinarian so close by." Reggie returned the man's firm handshake with one of her own. "In case Mr. Pibbs, her cat, ever gets sick."

"Call me Jake." The man's voice was so deep, it rumbled. "What breed is Mr. Pibbs?"

"Fluffy. Spoiled rotten." Reggie grinned. Mr. Pibbs had learned his way to the kitchen, where he invariably staked out a sunny spot to lie in while Nina cooked. "She rescued him from an alley when he was only a few days old. He's four."

"Spoiled kitties are my specialty," Jake said, his smile deepening. Turning to Michelle, he handed her a bottle of wine in a glossy gift bag. "Thanks for inviting me today. I've been curious about what was going to happen to this house and the property. I hated to think of it sitting here, vacant and moldering. Or worse."

Michelle's expression turned pensive. "It's such a beautiful old home. There are eight bed-rooms inside alone, and another full apartment out back. We think it would make a great inn. We're going to bring it up at Tuesday's town council meeting. I have my fingers crossed that we'll get the approval we need to move forward with our plans."

"Oh? I didn't know there was a proposal on the agenda." Jake's brow furrowed.

"Not officially," Michelle corrected. "But Mayor Maggie said we could have a few minutes to address the group before the meeting adjourns."

"I'll be there." Jake leaned closer, his voice dropping. "Town council meetings are about the most interesting thing that ever happens in Sugar Sand Beach. Everyone will be there. Come early if you want a good seat." His message delivered, he pulled himself erect. "I look forward to hearing your ideas."

"Feel free to wander through the house. I'm sure you'll see why we love it so," Michelle said, drawing the conversation to a close.

"Be sure to introduce yourself to Nina when you make your way to the kitchen," Reggie added. "And do help yourself to the appetizers. She's a world-class chef."

"Nice of him to tell us to come early," Michelle murmured as the vet moved off.

"It was," Reggie agreed. She expected Michelle

to hand her the hostess gift, the way she had with all the other plants, casseroles, bottles of wine and boxes of chocolate. Instead, she glanced through one of the door lites toward the parking area. For the first time since the open house had gotten underway, no new arrivals headed toward them.

"I don't think there's another person in Sugar Sand Beach, or within ten miles of here, who isn't already at our house," Michelle said with a tired laugh. Her shoulders slumped just a tad. "Would you mind taking over here for a while? I could use a break."

"Of course. Take as long as you want." Reggie pushed a sudden nervousness aside. She could handle this. Besides, Michelle deserved a chance to mingle a bit. Maybe her friend would even spend a few minutes chatting with Dave. The lawyer had been making the rounds for the past hour and a half. If the frequent glances he sent toward the entrance were any indication, she was the reason he'd stuck around as long as he had.

"Great." Paper crackled as Michelle hefted the wine bottle. "Where have you been putting these?"

"On the sideboard in the library. If there's no more room, stash it in the pantry." She'd already lined the top of the antique cabinet with enough bottles to stock a small wine cellar.

"Will do. I won't be long. If you need me, just give a shout." With that, Michelle's purposeful steps took her toward the other side of the house. She didn't get far, though. The women from the Ladies Auxiliary at the First Baptist Church of Sugar Sand Beach saw to that. According to Dave, the group had supplied meals and ferried Michelle's birth mother, Nancy, to and from doctor appointments for years. It was only natural they'd have questions for the new owner of their friend's house.

Reggie smiled softly when she spotted Dave lingering nearby. She wouldn't be one bit surprised if he whisked Michelle away from the group of women before long. She returned to her task and, for the next half-hour, Reggie chatted occasionally with a passing guest. A tiny, wizened woman who introduced herself as Polly Denton asked about the rose bushes by the front door. She teared up when Reggie told her the story of how they came to be there. The shouts and laughter of older kids who'd grown restless came from the backyard. Their play made Reggie doubly glad she'd closed and locked the out-buildings. Beyond the entrance hall, the hubbub of voices rose as neighbors and friends clumped together in groups of three or five to catch up on the events of the past week.

Reggie shot frequent looks through the glass door lite, but no additional guests pulled into the parking area before, with a fretful Hope in one arm and a diaper bag slung over the other shoulder, Chris stopped to say goodbye.

"I'd stay longer, but the little miss here is getting fussy. She's not used to so many people," he apologized.

"No, that's fine. Here." Reggie held the door open for him. She followed Chris onto the porch, determined to at least say hello to his daughter. "Is that better, sunshine?" she asked the baby once the door swung shut on the loud murmur of conversation coming from the house.

Hope buried her head in her daddy's shirt.

Reggie gulped. *Great.* Here she was risking heartache by being around Chris's daughter, and she couldn't even pry a smile from the child. She held up her hands, prepared to surrender.

"She likes to play peep-eye," Chris mouthed.

*Really?* Reggie lifted an eyebrow. When Chris nodded, she gave it a try.

"Peekaboo," she cooed. She covered her face with her hands. Peering through the gaps between her fingers, she grinned when the baby turned to look at her. "I see you," she said in a sing-song voice. She dropped her hands, and the little girl giggled.

The baby's laughter sent a liberal dose of happiness coursing through Reggie's veins. She smiled her thanks to Chris, then repeated the routine. This time, she blew Hope a kiss that caught the baby off-guard. The child's tiny mouth widened and her eyes blinked when Reggie's warm breath brushed her face. She giggled again and straightened in her father's arms. Reggie interpreted the move as an invitation to play some more.

More than happy to comply, Reggie repeated the simple game over and over. Sometimes she merely peered over her hands. Other times, she kept one eye hidden. Whenever she blew the baby a kiss, Hope gave her the same, startled look before the sweet sound of her giggles broke the silence. The child's laughter was infectious, and soon, both she and Chris laughed right along with little Hope.

Reggie was so captivated by the baby that she paid scant attention to a new arrival until a man's voice startled her.

"Well, isn't this a nice how-do-you-do. I drive all the way here from Virginia only to find my *wife* playing fast and loose with another man."

# Sixteen

## Reggie

*R*eggie froze the instant the harsh words reached her. Slowly, she swung her head toward the top of the steps, where the last person she'd expected to see today stood glowering at her. "Sam?" she asked.

Her gaze flew to the parking area and back. "Where did you come from?" She thought of an even more important question. "Why are you here?"

"I've come to take my wife home, of course." Sam edged closer.

Reggie's hands dropped to her sides. As if her feet had a mind of their own, they backed her away from the spot where Chris stood with his arms wrapped around his daughter. Stiffening, she shook her head. "We already had this conversation. You left. I don't want you back. It's over."

As if Hope sensed the sudden tension in the air, she whimpered softly. The game forgotten, the tiny girl once more buried her face in her father's shirt.

"Excuse me, but this sounds like a conversation my daughter doesn't need to hear." Hugging Hope close to his chest, Chris ducked back inside the house.

Reggie's stomach sank as she watched him go. Not that she blamed Chris for leaving. His first duty, after all, was to his child. But she sure could have used his support. Judging from Sam's firmly set jaw and the anger that flickered in her soon-to-be-ex's eyes, the man wasn't going to take a simple "No" for an answer. She squared her shoulders.

"Sam." Mindful of the house full of guests just a few feet away, she kept her voice low, her tone conciliatory. "This isn't a good time. We're in the middle of an open house. Half the town— well, all of it, to be honest—is inside. Maybe we could have this conversation another time? Another place?"

"I didn't drive all night and day to get here only for you to tell me this isn't a convenient time." Sam sneered, throwing her words back at her. His voice grew louder. "I don't care who hears me. It's time for you to come home. You've been gone a month. You've punished me enough. It's time for this to be over now."

Reggie eyed Sam carefully. For a man who'd spent the last eighteen hours behind the wheel, he looked awfully well put together. Not a trace of stubble graced his cheeks. Not a single wrinkle or stain marred the starched whiteness of his shirt. His slacks looked as though he'd just pulled them out of a dry cleaner's bag. Clearly, the man was lying about how he'd spent the past twenty-four hours, just as he'd lied about so many things. The secret bank accounts, the other woman—or women—in his life. She shook her head. There was a time when she'd have done just about anything for Sam, when she'd believed any lie he chose to tell her. But those days were over. Thanks to her friends, she was building a new life for herself. She was stronger now, and she wasn't going to give in to Sam's demands ever again.

Deliberately pitching her voice for his ears alone, she said, "Let me remind you, *you're* the one who walked out." He'd clearly forgotten who left who. "You're also the one who's been fooling around for...What? Three years? Longer?

Whatever. That makes me the wronged party. Not you. I'm the one who gets to decide when enough is enough. Not that it matters. I didn't come down here to punish you. I came to make a fresh start."

Sam glowered at her for several long beats. Though Reggie could practically see the steam coming out of his ears, he seemed to shrink into himself. Chinks appeared in his delivery as his shoulders rounded in what appeared to be defeat. "Fine." He waved a hand, dismissive. "Have it your way. Just come back with me. I—I need you," he begged.

Reggie took a breath. Sam had so much acting talent, he could have gone into theater. Instead, he'd chosen law. But she'd seen him practicing his courtroom theatrics in front of the mirror at their old apartment. It'd take a lot more than a few crocodile tears to fool her. "No, you don't," she said, her voice flat and emotionless. "You want something. What is it?"

As if he sensed his usual tricks wouldn't work anymore, Sam switched tactics. "You won't have to stay long. Six months. A year, tops," he wheedled. "Just till I nail down that partnership at the firm. After that, we can go our separate ways."

And there it was, the real reason Sam had

come after her. Reggie swallowed a laugh. She'd known all along he didn't want *her*. In his book, she was just a means to an end. He wanted his big chance at a promotion, and to get it, he had to prove to his family-friendly bosses that he was a happily married man. A fact he should have considered before he rented that suite at the Hilton. Or done any of a half dozen other things that proved she couldn't trust him. She gave her head an emphatic shake. "No. I'm telling you right now, as plainly as I can—It's. Over. Between. Us."

Dropping all pretense, Sam stared at her. His head swung from side to side like an angry bull's. His voice grew louder still until he was practically raving. "You don't know what you're talking about. You'd be lost without me. You have no skills. You can't support yourself. You're too stu—"

"That's quite enough!" Michelle snapped. She stepped onto the porch with Erin and Nina right on her heels. They were followed by Chris and Dave. The women fanned out around Reggie, while the men took up positions on either side of their unwelcome guest. "I believe Reggie has said all that's necessary," Michelle continued, using the tone that used to make Ashley and Aaron quake in their boots. "I'd appreciate it if you'd leave, Sam."

"We all would," added Erin. She brandished a clenched fist.

Reggie gently pressed down on her sister's raised arm. She held up one finger. "Before he leaves, I have something else to say." She crossed her arms over her chest. Scanning the faces around her, she drew strength from her friends, her sister. Finally, she addressed Sam. "For years, I listened to you tell me I wasn't worthy. That my work wasn't important. That *I* was the problem. When all along, you're the one who's been cheating, secretive, evasive. You have only yourself to blame for our divorce. To ask me to make a mockery of our marriage by coming back with you, well, that just isn't going to happen. Now leave, and don't come back. Or I'll file a restraining order. And then I'll make sure everyone at Shorter and Grominsky knows the truth."

"Hear, hear," Erin said at her left shoulder.

"Way to go, Reggie," Nina whispered from the other side.

"Dave, Chris." Michelle nodded to the parking area.

The two tall men nudged closer to Sam, their faces set in hard expressions.

"Let us walk you to your car," Dave suggested, his tone making it clear the matter wasn't up for discussion.

"Reggie, this is what you want?" Sam directed the question to Reggie, while the idea that he'd been defeated dawned across his flushed face.

"You betcha." She nodded.

Sam shook his head as if to clear it. "I never knew you had it in you." The barest hint of respect edged his voice. Looking at the two men who had taken positions on either side of him, he spared himself the indignity of getting hauled out to his car by pivoting on one heel. He marched smartly down the steps and across the lawn to the parking area, where a sedan sat cockeyed on the gravel. Chris and Dave matched him step for step.

"What do you think they're saying to him?" Michelle asked aloud, giving voice to the same question on Reggie's mind.

"I imagine they're making it very clear that no one in Sugar Sand Beach will put up with any more of his shenanigans," Nina ventured.

"And that he'd better not show his face around here again. Ever," Erin added.

They stood where they were, watching as Sam's car bumped down the graveled drive to the main street a few minutes later.

Reggie waited until Dave and Chris returned before she said, "Thanks, everyone. I appreciate y'all having my back."

"It was our pleasure," Dave said evenly. "If he gives you any more trouble, call me. I know a judge or two who wouldn't have any problem issuing an order of protection."

"Hopefully, it won't come to that." Reggie crossed her fingers. Sam was smart enough to realize that ending up on the wrong side of a restraining order was career suicide, wasn't he?

"I hated to leave you to face him alone, but I handed Hope off to Mom and rounded up the cavalry as fast as I could," Chris said. "Not that you needed it. You held your own pretty good."

"Oh, my goodness." Reggie stared at the window. On the other side of the glass, dozens of people milled about. "Do you think they heard all that?"

Michelle shrugged. "I imagine so. The way Sam was shouting, it was pretty hard to miss."

"Ack." Reggie buried her face in her hands. "I've ruined our open house. I'm so sorry."

"Nonsense," Nina said firmly. "You didn't ruin anything. That was all Sam's doing."

"But we probably ought to get back inside and do some damage control," Michelle suggested.

Reggie felt Erin's gaze on her. "What?"

"Are you really all right? Do you, um, need a minute?"

Reassuring her sister was one of the easiest things Reggie had ever done. "I'm fine. Better than fine, actually. I think that's the first time I've ever stood up to Sam. It felt good." She gave her sister a tight squeeze before they followed the rest of her men and women in shining armor into the house.

The minute they filed across the threshold, conversation, which had been buzzing before they walked in, ground to a halt. Everyone within sight turned their attention to the four hostesses.

Feeling like she was standing in the center of a spotlight—and not liking it one little bit— Reggie cleared her throat and stepped forward. "I'm so sorry you all had to be privy to my family drama. I hope that hasn't ruined your opinion of us."

Seconds ticked by. At last, the town's mayor spoke from the divan where she was seated. "Nonsense. We were beginning to think maybe y'all were too perfect for Sugar Sand Beach. Everybody here's got troubles of some sort. Seeing yours lets us know you'll fit right in here."

The group of women from the Ladies Auxiliary all nodded their heads in unison. Someone shouted out a hearty, "Amen!" A few others rumbled, "Way to go," and "Atta girl."

In her crisp chef's whites, Nina piped up. "There's still tons of food in the kitchen, folks, including some of the best pound cake I've ever tasted. Please don't let all this food go to waste."

And just like that, the awkwardness faded. Conversation began to flow again. Nina drafted Erin to help her in the kitchen. Hoping for a bite of this and a taste of that, several of their guests followed them. Michelle took small groups on private tours, where she pointed out the improvements and changes they hoped to make before opening the inn.

Meanwhile, Reggie found Chris and played another round or two of peekaboo with Hope. As she walked the single dad and his daughter to the door a little bit later, she thanked the man who was rapidly earning a spot on her short list of good friends.

That evening, after the last guest had departed, the leftovers had been wrapped and stored, and they'd gone through the house disposing of discarded glasses and plates, Reggie, Erin and Michelle gathered on the front porch. Above them, stars twinkled in the clear, black sky. Crickets chirped from the nearby bushes. An owl hooted in the distance.

"Somebody get the door, will ya?" Nina called from inside.

"Got it." Erin, who was sitting the closest, reached for the handle.

Carrying a pitcher filled with yummy Gulf Coast Sunset, the inn's signature drink, and four tall glasses, Nina joined the others. She crossed directly to the glass-topped table.

"I don't know about the rest of you, but I intend to sleep in tomorrow. I'm bushed," Michelle said as she accepted the glass Nina handed her. "Anybody know what time church services are down here?"

"I think every one of those women from the Baptist Church made a point of telling me they have two services—at nine thirty and eleven." Nina sank onto one of the wicker chairs. "I'm going to spend some quality time with Mr. Pibbs first thing. Even though I kept my door shut, having all the people in the house scared him. He's still hiding under the bed. But if you want to catch the 11 o'clock, I'm in."

"It's a date." Michelle drank deeply.

"That'll give me time to take one of the kayaks out for a while before we go." Erin took a swallow and licked her lips. She turned to her sister. "How about you, Reggie? Are you game?"

"Sure." Reggie flexed her arms. "I could use some time on the water." It had been years since she and Erin had paddled out together.

"I hope everyone likes casseroles, because we'll be eating those for the next week or two." Wicker complained softly as Nina shifted in her chair, trying to get comfortable.

"I'd heard about Southern hospitality, but I never in my wildest dreams expected so much food," Michelle said with a smile.

"Or potted plants. Or wine," Reggie added.

"I put a half dozen dishes in the freezer, and that doesn't count the ones we served today."

"Or the pound cakes," Erin said. "How many of those are left?"

"Three. We'll never eat them all." Nina flexed her fingers.

"Speak for yourself." Erin crossed her ankles. "I had a slice earlier today. If they're all as good as the one I tried, they'd be great for breakfast."

"So…" Michelle searched their faces. "How do you think everything went today? Anyone overhear complaints? Problems?"

"I didn't hear a single negative word," Nina said. "A bunch of people asked me for recipes. I told them we'd put all their favorites on the menu at the café." She cupped her chin. "Once we've been open for a while, I might think about writing a cookbook. *Recipes From The Sugar Sand Inn.* How does that sound?"

"Great." Erin smiled. "But let's make sure there is a Sugar Sand Inn first."

"Everyone I talked to was really positive about saving the house by turning it into an inn." Reggie brushed a hand through her hair. "But then Sam showed up, and I really thought he'd blown our chance for us."

"But that turned out surprisingly okay." Erin took another sip of her drink.

"Well, I think, despite Sam's appearance—or maybe because of it—we made a good first impression on the people of Sugar Sand Beach." Michelle lifted her glass in a toast. "Next up, the town council meeting on Tuesday night."

Glasses clinked and cheers were raised as the four friends determined to put their best foot forward at the council meeting, where the fate of the Sugar Sand Inn would be decided.

# Seventeen

## Erin

Sunday morning, Erin wiggled her toes in the beach's fine, sugary sand. Cool and moist, the grains shifted beneath her weight. A tiny wave, little more than a ripple, washed ashore. It deposited a piece of red sea glass at her feet before retreating. Not one to ignore a good omen, she picked up the gift and tucked it into the pocket of her board shorts for safekeeping.

She scanned the sky. In the east, the first rays of sunlight had turned low-hanging clouds a brilliant gold. A salty breeze brushed softly against her face. The Gulf, much calmer, much quieter than the ocean, called to her. Her fingers twitched with a longing to feel the handle of a paddle.

Where was Reggie?

They'd agreed to meet at six thirty. It was nearly that now. Eager to get on the water, she'd already lugged both kayaks down from the house. They sat, noses pointing toward the Gulf, ready for their first voyage in years. She dug in her pocket and rubbed her fingers along the smooth edges of the glass, hoping both of the boats were as seaworthy as she thought they were. If they weren't, today's outing would be far too short.

At last, she heard someone coming down the path to the beach. With a brief turn of her head, she spotted her sister a few yards away from the spot where the tall sea grass ended. Reggie had worn a loose T-shirt over jean shorts. Erin's lips twisted. She had tons of rash guards and board shorts. The next time they took the kayaks out, she'd offer a set to her sister. Designed to dry quickly, the close-fitting clothes were ideal for paddlers.

"Hey, I would've helped with the kayaks," Reggie said, stepping onto the beach.

"You know me. I like to get an early start on things." It was both an asset and a curse.

"You're late if you're on time." Reggie repeated one of Erin's favorite mantras.

"Yeah." She chuckled.

"Looks like a good day for a paddle." Reggie clapped her hands and rubbed them together. Her gaze landed on the small pile of equipment stacked on one end of the largest kayak. "Do we have to wear life jackets? I mean, I can swim, you know."

"Never go on the water without a PFD." The personal floatation devices were like seat belts. People never thought they'd need one, but when they did, they were mighty glad they were buckled in.

Erin took two vests off the pile and handed one to her sister. Once they'd slipped them on and zippered them up, she eyed her sister's sandals. The straps were apt to hang up in the kayak's foot well. "Do you need a pair of booties?" She'd brought extras just in case.

"I wouldn't mind. I was planning to go barefoot, but these will be better," Reggie said as she kicked off her sandals. Perched on the kayak, she slipped her feet into the soft-soled rubber shoes.

"You remember how to do this?" Years had passed since the last time the two of them had kayaked together.

"I might be a little rusty," Reggie admitted, "but I'm sure it'll all come back to me."

"Okay, then." Erin shook her head. "I wish

we had two sea-going kayaks, but we're stuck with these until I bring my own back from the Keys." The two boats sitting in front of them had been among the many items Michelle had inherited from Nancy Simmons. The saltwater craft was long and sleek, while the one made for freshwater looked more like a fat cigar. It alone featured a foot well, and with its wider beam, was less likely to tip over. She motioned Reggie to the more stable craft. If anyone got dunked on this trip, she didn't want it to be her sister.

"About twenty yards offshore, the water gets plenty deep." Erin had checked the depth charts before she turned in last night. "We'll head east, follow the coast past the Topsail Hill Preserve. Then circle back. A little over six miles altogether. Sound good?" The trip wasn't a long one, but it'd give them a good workout. They'd never get too far from the spot where they'd launched, an added plus when using unfamiliar craft.

"I'm game," Reggie said with a grin. She moved to the front of her kayak, took hold of the grab handle and headed for the water while Erin did the same.

They waded knee-deep into the gentle surf, plunked their butts into the cockpits of their watercraft and swung their feet into position straight out in front of them. Almost as if they'd practiced the move, they picked up their double-sided paddles at the same time and aimed for deeper water.

Erin quickly settled into a familiar rhythm, her arms bicycling as she dipped and pulled with one side of the paddle, then the other. At first, she hung back a bit, watching Reggie carefully, ready to offer advice or even haul her sister back to shore, if necessary. But when the other kayak sliced through the water nearly as effortlessly as her own, she took a deep breath and settled in to enjoy their journey.

Gentle waves sloshed against the sides of the boats. Below them, the bottom fell away, the water color changing from nearly translucent to a crystal-clear blue green. Reggie's turn was a little awkward, but she dug deeper on the ocean side, and soon they were headed east along the shore. The breeze stiffened slightly as they paddled into the wind. Erin smiled as Reggie paused to clamp her baseball cap a little lower on her head.

"Hello, little fellow." Reggie leaned over the water for a closer look at a black diving bird that had surfaced near her kayak.

"A cormorant," Erin called. She'd run across the fishing birds frequently in her travels. They ranged throughout the United States and as far south as Central America.

"It's an anhinga," Reggie corrected with no trace of the hesitancy Erin had grown used to hearing. "No hooked beak. This one's male. See those white feathers?"

Erin nodded. So it was, she thought, just as the bird dove beneath the water's surface. Staying well out of range of their paddles, he kept pace with the kayaks while he fished for his morning's breakfast.

Along the shore, sand dunes led to wide, sloping beaches. "That's where the Topsail Hill Preserve starts," Erin called. Early sailors had sworn the dunes reminded them of their ships' topsails, and the name had stuck.

Reggie rested her paddle crossways on her kayak. She pointed to the shore, where a small herd of deer trotted down the face of a sandy dune. The youngsters in the group frolicked at the water's edge while the older does meandered down the beach. "You don't see that every day."

"No, you sure don't," Erin agreed. They sat, treading water until the deer neared a man who sat in a beach chair, a tall fishing pole in his hand. His presence made the animals nervous, and when he stood suddenly, the movement startled them. The entire herd fled, racing up one of the dunes and disappearing down the other side in the blink of an eye.

Erin had just picked up her paddle when an enormous stingray swam under their kayaks. The water was so clear, they could see the sharp barbs that stuck out from its whip-like tail.

"Yikes," Reggie called. "I wouldn't want to make him angry."

"They're more afraid of you than you are of them." Most creatures were. Erin could think of a few exceptions. Only people with death wishes ventured close to orcas, polar bears or hippos. However, there wasn't much chance of running into one of those this close to the sunny Gulf shore. There were other dangers, and she made a note to remind her sister and the others that rays often buried themselves in the sand in shallow water. By doing the Stingray Shuffle, they could avoid stepping on a barb. Which stung like the Dickens. She should know. She'd been stung a time or two while working in the Keys.

They'd been paddling for over an hour when houses began to crowd the once-pristine shoreline. "We've reached the end of the preserve," Erin called. "Time to head back." She turned her kayak in a wide arc and was glad to see that Reggie had no trouble negotiating the U-turn. Once both boats were pointed in the opposite direction, she safed her paddle, grabbed two water bottles from under her hatch. She took a long drink from one and tossed the other to her sister.

"You doing okay?" she asked as Reggie snagged the bottle.

"Great. This is the most fun I've had in a long while." Reggie removed her hat from her head and wiped a sheen of sweat from her brow. She downed half her water. "We need to do this more often."

"We will," Erin promised. She stowed her bottle and picked up her paddle. A low bank of gray clouds had formed in the west. She lifted her chin toward the approaching storm. "We want to be off the water before that gets here."

"Race ya," Reggie called, grinning. She didn't wait for Erin's answer but dug her paddle into the water and took off.

Erin laughed. Reggie's blunt-nosed model was no match for her streamlined saltwater kayak, but she had to give her sister credit. Reggie's paddle whirled as the younger girl pushed through a light chop. To make it a fair fight, Erin waited a full minute before following. For a while, she thought she might have given Reggie too much of a head start. She had to work hard to catch up and harder still to stay abreast of the other boat. Especially after a pod of playful dolphins appeared to join in the fun. In slightly deeper water, the gray mammals raced alongside the pair of kayaks. For most of the way back, they dove and swam beside them, their sleek silver bodies glistening whenever they surfaced for air. Just before Reggie and Erin reached their launching spot, though, the pod made an abrupt turn and headed for deeper water.

"Whew! That was a blast." Reggie stripped off her wading shoes after they'd beached the kayaks on the sand. "I'm going to be sore tomorrow, though." She stretched her arms to the sides.

"You looked great out there. Like you'd kayaked every day of your life," Erin said.

"It was good to do something different for a change. I'm glad you suggested it. After yesterday, what with Sam and all, I needed a break."

A sudden concern rushed through Erin. Her sister had been through a lot lately. "You doing okay? Be honest." When her marriage to Ron had broken up, it had taken her a good, long while to pull herself back together. And their divorce had been an amicable one. She could only imagine what Reggie was going through.

Reggie sank down on the sand. "It hasn't been easy. I'll admit there have been days when I didn't want to get out of bed. But finding out

I wasn't to blame took away a lot of the pain. Plus, having you and the others to turn to, that's really made a huge difference."

Erin pursed her lips. She just plain didn't like Sam. Never had. And after what happened yesterday, she never would. But heaping blame on the man wouldn't help her sister heal. Drawing from her own experience, she gave Reggie the best advice she had to offer. "The thing is, no matter how hurtful and deceitful Sam turned out to be, at one point, you loved him. You need to give yourself space to grieve that lost love." For her, that had led to over twenty years of bouncing from place to place. She wanted better for Reggie.

"I hear you. And I intend to." Reggie clapped the pair of booties together. Sand sifted down from them. She slipped her feet into her sandals. "As strange as it sounds, that's one of the reasons why I'm glad our divorce won't be final for six months. It gives me time, you know. To figure out where I go from here."

"You think you'll leave?" She hoped not. Not only couldn't she imagine running the Sugar Sand Inn without Reggie, she wanted to be close to her sister.

"Nah. That part's a no-brainer." Reggie chuckled. "I can't think of anything I'd rather do than be a part of all this." With a sweep of her hand, she gestured beyond the beach to the house.

Happiness flooded Erin. "Me, too, little sister," she whispered. "Me, too."

# Eighteen

## Michelle

*I*n the passenger seat of her SUV, Michelle ran a self-conscious hand over the narrow pencil skirt that went with the smartly tailored suit jacket she'd chosen to wear to the town council meeting. Should she have worn a dress instead? What if everyone else showed up in jeans—would she look like she was trying too hard? She clucked her tongue.

She should have asked Maggie Henson about the dress code, but she'd been so busy with every-thing else—preparing for the open house, practicing her presentation, reviewing the business plan—that she hadn't given what to wear to the meeting a moment's thought until she was standing in front of her closet wrapped in a towel, her shoulders still wet from the shower. In the end, she'd selected the suit because it had been one of Allen's favorites. Plus, it conveyed the professional image she was trying to portray rather than the frowsy-housewife look she'd sported all last year.

"Quit fidgeting. You look amazing," Erin said from behind the wheel.

Trust Erin to know what she was thinking. They'd been friends so long, the woman could read her like a book. But she had to agree—the suit did look good on her. The fifteen pounds she'd fretted over had simply melted off in the move. Best of all, they'd taken another five along with them. As a result, the slim-fitting outfit looked better on her now than it did the day she bought it.

"You don't think maybe I should have worn something less, um, stuffy?" she asked. She played with one of the pearl studs Allen had given her for their twentieth wedding anniversary.

"Relax. You saw the crowd at the open house. And again at church Sunday." People had shown up at both events dressed in everything from come-as-you-are casual to Friday-night date night. "Anything goes in Sugar Sand Beach."

Michelle took a deep breath. "Okay," she said on the slow exhale. "You look nice yourself, I might add." Erin had paired a beaded bolero top with white dress slacks.

"Thanks. I picked this up in Spain. It's one of my favorites." Taking one hand off the wheel, she trailed her fingers over the intricate stitching.

"Hey, how about us? We're not exactly slobs back here," Reggie piped up.

Michelle adjusted the mirror on her visor so she had a better view of the back seat. "You're both perfect," she declared and meant it. Reggie's tanned arms and face glowed against the olive-green shirtwaist that also brought out the subtle shades of red in her hair. Nina, meanwhile, had gone for an artsy look, with a lightweight tulle dress that flared out from narrow shoulders to form a bell-shaped hem at mid-calf.

"If we looked any better, they'd sell tickets," Nina declared dryly. "I'm more concerned about everyone's reaction to our proposal. Have we gotten any calls from people who came to the open house?"

"I didn't tell you? Oh, my goodness!" Michelle gasped. "I'd say my phone has been ringing off the hook but, you know, it's a cell phone." She laughed. "Seriously, I've probably had twenty calls congratulating us on throwing what one of the ladies from church called 'the party of the year.' Everyone's been so positive."

"Don't you think it's odd that Orson Danner didn't stop by on Saturday? I thought he would—if for no other reason than to tell us how foolish we were." Erin turned onto Sugar Sand Beach's main street. Cars and trucks filled the parking spaces on both sides. She whistled under her breath. It was a good thing they'd come early.

"That's the guy Dave was talking about. The developer, right?" Reggie asked from the back seat.

"Yeah. And speak of the devil, there he is now." Erin aimed her chin toward a figure emerging from a black sedan.

"Well, that answers that question." Michelle sighed. She'd been hoping Orson would skip the meeting. So much for that. She studied the man who ambled down the sidewalk like he owned the street. The black shirt and pants he'd worn, combined with his jet-black hair and pale complexion, reminded her of the Elvis impersonators she'd seen on a trip to Las Vegas. "I just hope he doesn't stir up trouble."

"Don't worry," Nina coached. "You inherited Nancy's property fair and square. He can't force us to sell it."

"That's the thing," Michelle reminded every-one. "We might have to if the council doesn't

approve the re-zoning or our plans for the inn."
With so much at stake tonight, no wonder her
hands trembled. She clasped them tightly on her
lap.

The sobering effect of her words silenced the
group as Erin drove past the line of parked cars
and finally slid into an empty space five doors
down from the community center. As she
stepped from the car, Michelle couldn't wrench
her thoughts away from all they'd lose if council
turned down their proposal. She froze, thinking
hard.

She didn't want to sell her birthright—the
house and the land Nancy Simmons had left
her—any more than she wanted to see the house
razed, dozens of tiny homes built in its place. But
none of them could afford to stay in Sugar Sand
Beach on their own.

Oh, if they all got jobs and chipped in
together, they might be able to maintain the
house and grounds. For a while, at least. A year.
Maybe two. But property taxes and insurance
would eat up their savings before too long. No, if
the council turned them down, they'd have no
choice. They'd have to sell out. To Orson or
another developer like him.

And then what?

They'd scatter to the four winds, that's what.

Nina would head back to Virginia, where jobs were plentiful. The water called to Erin; she'd either settle down in her little cottage in the Keys or go back to wandering the globe. The bond between Reggie and her sister had strengthened to the point where wherever one headed, the other would probably follow. As for herself, she loved it right here. She wanted to make Sugar Sand Beach her home, with or without her birth mother's inheritance. But the thought of the four of them going their separate ways brought tears to her eyes.

*It wouldn't come to that, would it?*

Not if she had anything to say about it, it wouldn't. Her hand on the hood of the car, she gave herself a pep talk. With Dave's help and guidance, she'd plugged every hole in their business plan. She'd rehearsed her little speech so often she could recite it in her sleep. In fact, last night she'd dreamed of standing at the podium tonight, delivering a flawless talk.

"Focus on the positive. We've got this," Reggie said, her voice cutting through Michelle's brain freeze like a hot knife through butter.

"You're right." She needed to focus on the positive. Not failure but success.

Squaring her shoulders, Michelle joined the other three on the sidewalk. Bolstered by her friends' confidence, she linked arms with Erin, while Reggie and Nina did the same behind them. The four of them walked two by two through the double doors of the Sugar Sand Beach Community Center.

Michelle wasn't quite sure what to expect inside. A tasteful entryway, perhaps. Certainly a reception desk with information about activities and businesses in the area. Maybe a large room with a raised dais where the town council would conduct its business. A podium.

Yeah, this place offered none of those things. If she had to compare the center to something, she'd have to say it was more like walking into a gymnasium than anything else. Flyers and business cards dotted a couple of bulletin boards mounted on the walls just inside the door. One end of the hall sported a huge, electronic bingo board. Straight ahead, curtains were drawn closed across a small stage. On the floor beneath it, someone had set up several long, folding tables. Like placemats, seven pads of paper sat evenly spaced on the tabletops, one for every member of the council. While a gavel and a microphone sat beside the centermost pad, every place setting featured a bottle of water and an ink pen. Metal folding chairs arranged in wavy lines filled the rest of the large space. Despite their arrival a good forty-five minutes before the meeting, about half the chairs were already occupied.

"I guess we'd better find seats," Erin whispered over the mix of conversation, the scrape of chair legs, the sound of doors opening and closing.

"Look for four on the aisle," Michelle directed. She scanned for empty spots.

"There." Nina pointed to a group of empty chairs near the front.

"Perfect." Following the chef's lead, Michelle headed in that direction.

But she'd no sooner started toward the chairs when her progress was halted by one of the women she recognized from the open house. Not wanting to appear rude on this night, of all nights, she and Erin stopped to chat. They spent a good ten minutes exchanging greetings, first with her and then with various business owners. By the time they joined Reggie and Nina, who'd forged on through the crowd to reserve their seats, a steady stream of citizens of Sugar Sand Beach filed in through the double doors, and the mayor and council members had taken their places up front.

At precisely seven o'clock, Mayor Maggie Henson gave the microphone three quick taps. Michelle swallowed hard as the noise level in the room rose while stragglers rushed to their seats.

The mayor gave everyone a minute or two to get settled before, with a bang of the gavel, she welcomed them all to the town council meeting. She then turned the floor over to a minister from the Church of The Rock, who offered a brief convocation.

Once the man in the ill-fitting suit finished and slipped quietly out a side door, the mayor addressed the group. "Normally, we'd hear from the finance officer and secretary next, but tonight we have the privilege of honoring our local high school graduates." She smiled broadly while a few people clapped. "At this time, I'd like our graduates to come forward." She beckoned toward the front row.

There was a rustle of movement, a false start or two, and at last, six young people rose from their chairs. They lined up, facing the crowd. Applause thundered through the room as a high school teacher who lived in Sugar Sand Beach read each graduate's name. The group then filed past the line of council members, who shook their hands. Standing at the end of the row, the Town Treasurer handed each young adult a check for $100. Afterward, another round of applause filled the room while the smiling teens quickly filed out the same side door the minister had used.

The room quieted again. The mayor moved to the next item on the agenda—a yawn-inducing financial report from the town treasurer. Michelle had trouble keeping her eyes open through the secretary's reading of the minutes, but she perked up a bit as they moved on to a proposal that would prevent trucks or vans with commercial signage from parking in residential areas.

Unlike recognizing the high school graduates, which had received unanimous approval, this idea sparked a somewhat heated debate. The people who favored the new rule apparently owned more expensive homes in the area. However, the majority of Sugar Sand Beach's citizens either drove such vehicles themselves or had family members who did. Maggie allowed each speaker two minutes to say their piece and employed her gavel liberally to keep things moving. When it finally came time to vote on the measure, the council struck it down five to two.

Several less contentious items of business followed until Maggie finally announced the last thing on the agenda—a proposal to double the size of the smoke house at the Sugar Sand Beach Grocery Store.

A lanky man stood from his seat in the

middle of the room. "Madam Mayor," he called.

"Note in the minutes that the mayor recognizes Jimbo Dutton, owner of the Sugar Sand Gas & Oil," Maggie responded.

Jimbo pulled on his jaw. Sounding anything but serious, he said, "I object to this here proposal to build a bigger smoke house. The smell of Gus's sausages already makes me so hungry, I have to close up shop every day right at noon to buy one. If he's smokin' more of 'em over there, I'm gonna have to get two. I'll get fat."

Michelle and the others joined in the laughter that rippled through the room as Jimbo doffed an imaginary hat in Gus's direction. Grinning broadly, the service station owner plopped back down onto his seat.

Chuckling and shaking her head, Maggie tapped the table with her gavel. "All right, all right. Settle down, everyone." She paused for a few seconds while the last of the laughter died out. Without missing a beat, she said, "Thank you very much for your comment, Jimbo. Is there any additional, perhaps more pertinent, discussion of this matter?"

When there wasn't, the council approved Gus's proposal without a dissenting vote while Michelle's stomach gurgled happily. It sounded like everyone in Sugar Sand Beach liked the grocery store's smoked sausage as much as she did.

But now that the meeting was winding down, she tensed. Any time now, Maggie would strike her gavel and give her the floor. Could she convince everyone here to give her—to give all four of them—a chance?

Sure enough, tap, tap, tap went the gavel a few seconds later. The mayor lifted an eyebrow in her direction. Though her fingers shook, Michelle returned the mayor's unspoken question with a slight nod. She was as ready as she'd ever be.

"Before we adjourn this evening, Ms. Robinson, the new owner of Nancy Simmons's property, would like to bring a concern before us," Maggie said, once more addressing the entire group. "I've granted her five minutes to speak. Afterwards, we'll open the floor for discussion for ten minutes. Ms. Robinson."

Michelle rose on trembling legs. But trembling was good. With so much at stake and so much responsibility resting on her shoulders, she supposed she should be glad she could stand at all. But as she looked out over the crowded seats, a calm descended over her. The people who'd come to the town council meeting were her neighbors, her friends. She'd shopped at many of their businesses. They'd been to her house. She didn't need to impress them with fancy speeches. She just needed to appeal to them as one neighbor to another.

And so she did.

"Thank you for letting me speak tonight, Ms. Mayor, council members," she began. "I may not have lived in Sugar Sand Beach for very long, but I instantly fell in love with this town, with its people. I want to preserve its sense of community…" She spoke for the full five minutes about her hope that by converting the house left to her by Nancy Simmons into an inn—with a café—she and her friends could provide jobs for local residents and let tourists experience a real taste of Florida life.

When she'd finished, she opened the floor to questions and braced herself.

As expected, Orson Danner practically flew out of his seat. "Ms. Robinson, my corporation has millions of dollars to invest in this area. Not only that, we have certified contractors, architects, builders and planners working for us. Instead of all we intend to bring to Sugar Sand Beach, you want to open a mom-and-pop inn. Tell us, do you even have any experience in the hospitality industry?"

Michelle took a breath. She found Dave's face

in the crowd and smiled. The challenge was one they had prepared for. She answered Orson's question honestly. "No. Not directly, I don't. However, I have a business degree from the University of Virginia, and between myself and my three friends, we feel confident we can make this work." She fanned through a copy of the detailed business plan she'd provided to all of the council members earlier in the week. "As you can see, we have the resources to cover the repairs and minor remodeling needed in order to bring the inn up to code. In addition, we have enough cash reserves to see us through the first year of operations."

"Huh." Orson folded his arms across his beefy chest. "Just so you know, Ms. Robinson, any offers we've made on property in and about Sugar Sand Beach are contingent on acquiring the Simmons, pardon me, your land. If you somehow do get the council to rezone the property and approve your plan, we'll rescind all those offers. By the time your little inn goes belly up, we'll have invested our money somewhere else."

*Well, that wasn't piling on the pressure…much.*

Michelle thought Orson had missed his calling. Give the man a set of thumbscrews and he'd have made a world-class torturer in the

Middle Ages. But he was wrong if he thought she'd succumb to his tactics.

Forcing every bit of self-confidence she had—and some she didn't—into her tone, she firmed her voice. "We won't fail, Mr. Danner." She turned toward the seated council. "If the council gives us permission to move forward, that is."

There wasn't much more Orson could say. As Erin had pointed out earlier, he might have had big plans for the Simmons property, but now that it belonged to Michelle, there was only so much he could do. While Orson stewed, she fielded a couple of easy questions from the assembly.

At the ten-minute mark, Maggie once more tapped her gavel. "Ms. Robinson, thank you for your insightful presentation." She scanned the faces of the council members on either side of her. "Do I hear a motion that we vote on rezoning Ms. Robinson's property and granting the approval she needs to open the Sugar Sand Inn at our next—"

Michelle's brow furrowed as Maggie's voice cut off in mid-sentence. Cupping her hand over the mic, the mayor leaned in for a hushed conversation with Polly Denton, the woman who owned a small flower shop on the main street. Maggie continued holding her hand over the mic as the other board members chimed in. At last, she pinned Michelle with a searching look.

"Ms. Robinson, the council would prefer to vote on this matter tonight," the mayor announced. "Would you have any objections?"

*Say what?*

Michelle swallowed…hard. This wasn't the way it was supposed to go. They were supposed to have another month to sweet-talk the members of the council, to win over the townspeople and to prove they were Sugar Sand Beach material. In her heart, though, she knew that, no matter what she and Erin and Nina and Reggie did between now and the next town council meeting, these people had already made up their minds. There was no point in delaying the inevitable, no matter which way the council voted.

She scanned the faces of her friends and saw that they'd reached the same conclusion. Throwing caution to the wind, she answered for all of them. "No, Madam Mayor. We'd welcome the council's decision."

Maggie tapped her pencil on the table. "This is rather out of the ordinary." Dropping her pencil, she straightened. "I'll need a motion from the floor. Do I hear one?"

Moving pretty fast for a man his size, Gus

jumped to his feet. "Madam Mayor, I make a motion that the council approve the application of Ms. Robinson to open the Sugar Sand Inn and Café in the house formerly known as the Simmons residence."

Jake Stewart rose a bit more slowly. "I second that motion."

Giving her gavel quite the workout, Maggie banged it again. "In that case, council members, what say you? All in favor?"

In the long pause that followed, Michelle's heart hammered in her chest. First Reggie, then Erin and Nina, rose to stand at her side. Arms around each other's waists, they leaned on each other while the seven people seated in front of them decided their fates. They didn't have to wait long.

From the far end of the table, Polly Denton called, "Aye." A veritable chorus of "Ayes" followed.

"Let the record show Ms. Robinson's application for re-zoning has been granted. Furthermore, the council gives its wholehearted approval for the Sugar Sand Inn and Café," Maggie said when the final vote had been cast. A broad smile broke across the mayor's face. She picked up her gavel one final time and struck the table. "Meeting adjourned," she called.

Michelle's legs went out from under her, and she sank onto her chair. She couldn't believe their good luck. Reggie, Nina and Erin crowded close. Each wore an expression of profound happiness.

"I want to kick up my heels and dance for joy," Erin whispered.

"Let's save that for when we get home." Michelle surveyed the room. A few people had left, but most lingered to chat. Some were slowly making their way toward them. "For now, we need to thank our neighbors and friends for making our dream a reality."

They fanned out, shaking hands and exchanging hugs with people who offered their congratulations. After she'd spoken to Dave and invited him to join them back at the house in a little while, Michelle made a special point of seeking out Polly Denton.

"I so appreciate what you did, bringing our proposal to a vote like that," she said to the tiny woman. "Never in my wildest dreams did I think we'd get approval for the inn tonight."

"It was the story about your roses that did it," Polly declared.

"My roses?" Michelle brushed her hair behind one ear. Had she heard that right?

"That nice Miss Reggie told me how much your late husband—God rest his soul—loved those rose bushes. And how when you saw them there on the porch, you said you were home. That flat brought tears to my eyes. And I just knew you and your friends were the kind of people we need here in Sugar Sand Beach." The lines around the octogenarian's face deepened into a warm smile. "I'm so glad it turned out the way it did for you girls." She waved to someone behind Michelle. "I have to run. My ride's ready—I don't drive at night anymore. Y'all stop by the flower shop soon, now, y'hear?"

"Yes, ma'am." Michelle offered the easy assurance before Polly hurried off. For a second, she rocked back on her heels, awed by how Reggie's kindness had impacted all their lives.

Later, when they'd piled into the SUV, Michelle finally let go of the squeal of joy she'd been holding in. "Can you believe it?" she gushed. "We did it!"

"When they said they were going to put it to a vote right then, I thought I'd faint," Nina said.

"This is the best news, the absolute best," Reggie cried.

"Let's go home and open up a bottle of the good stuff. We deserve it!" Erin carefully backed out of the parking space.

"Sounds good to me." Michelle leaned her head against the headrest. The coming months would bring new challenges, new obstacles to overcome, but confidence flowed through her veins. Nothing could stop them now that they had the town council's approval. She closed her eyes. Tears dampened her cheeks as their dream of opening the Sugar Sand Inn moved one giant step closer to reality.

# Nineteen

## Reggie

Reggie sat on the front steps, her back pressed against the sturdy, wrought-iron railing Chris had installed. She propped the thick manila envelope that had arrived in today's mail in her lap. The package bore her attorney's return address. Hoping against hope the envelope held what she'd been waiting for, she crossed her fingers. Laughing at herself, she uncrossed them just as quickly. Opening the package required both hands.

Thick, yellow paper crackled as she ripped the flap and peered inside. Her heart thudding, she withdrew a sheaf of papers. The line at the top of the first page read, "Marital Separation Agreement." Reggie dropped the papers back into her lap with a sigh.

Her marriage was as good as done. True to his word—for once—Sam had signed the agreement soon after he returned to Virginia. He'd even gone a step further and filled out an affidavit swearing he wouldn't contest the divorce and—more importantly—relinquished all claim to Reggie's future earnings. The move paved the way for her to become a full-fledged partner in Sugar Sand Inn. In exchange, she'd asked for a lump sum payment in lieu of alimony, or as her attorney called it, spousal support. A white business envelope clipped to the rest of the papers held the check. She slipped it out. Taking a pen from her back pocket, she glanced briefly at the amount and scrawled her name across the back. After returning the check to the envelope, she carefully tucked both it and the pen into the pocket of her jean shorts.

Wondering if Sam had included a note now that she'd insisted they only communicate through her attorney, she thumbed through the rest of the papers. But there was nothing. No note. No letter written in Sam's heavy script.

She let out a long, slow breath. He hadn't apologized. But she could live with that. She hadn't needed or expected him to say he was sorry for lying to her for as long as he had. Not really. No, if the breakup of her marriage had taught her one thing, it was that she wasn't responsible for Sam's bad behavior. His problems were all his own, and from here on out, that's how he could deal with them…on his own.

Looking out over the sea grass and the path that led down to Sugar Sand Beach, Reggie took a minute to examine her heart. Much like noxious plants reacted when she treated them with weed killer, the hurt and anger she'd felt after Sam's betrayal had withered under the advice and support she'd received from Erin, Nina and Michelle. She had to admit that, in his own quiet way, Chris had helped, too.

Sure, she still had some work to do. She'd spent over five years trying and failing to live up to Sam's expectations. The experience had left her with a healthy crop of self-doubt. She was ripping it out, bit by bit, but she couldn't expect it to go away overnight. And yeah, once in a while, a whiff of self-pity would blow through her soul. Until she got rid of that, she certainly wouldn't be ready for a new relationship. But she suspected that by the time Christmas rolled around and her divorce was final, she might be. She smiled. When the time came, who knew? Maybe her friendship with Chris would deepen into something more.

At a metallic click, Reggie reeled in her

wandering thoughts. Her smile widened as the front door swung open. One by one, Michelle and Erin stepped onto the porch. Reggie scrambled to her feet when Nina emerged from the house carrying a heavy tray a few minutes later.

"Hey, is it that time already?" she asked. Ever since the town council had granted their request, the four of them had gathered on the front porch each evening. While they watched the sunset, they filled each other in on the progress they'd made that day and their plans for the next. Most evenings, Nina fixed tall glasses of perfectly sweetened iced tea, but on Saturdays, they celebrated the end of another week in paradise with a pitcher of the inn's signature drink, the Gulf Coast Sunset.

While Michelle and Erin made themselves comfortable in the white wicker chairs, Reggie helped serve the drinks. She passed around napkins along with a basket of crisp, round crackers Nina had thoughtfully provided. Settling into her own chair, Reggie bit into one of the crackers. A tangy, cheesy taste with a nice peppery kick filled her mouth. "Oh," she said, grinning at Nina. "These are great! Make sure you hang on to this recipe."

"You like them?" Nina beamed. Mr. Pibbs had made himself at home on her chair. She lifted him off the cushion, sank onto it herself, and settled him in her lap before she continued. "They're pretty simple, actually, but they're one of my favorites."

"There's no better way to end the week than with a yummy drink, the perfect snack and great company," Erin declared.

"Don't forget the sunset." Michelle nodded to the western sky, where the setting sun had turned a bank of low clouds into burnished gold.

Reggie dug the thin white envelope out of her pocket. Leaning forward, she pressed it into Michelle's hand.

"What's this?" Michelle's eyebrows lifted.

"My divorce settlement. There was twenty thou left after I paid Mr. Cole." She nodded to Erin. Much as she appreciated her sister's offer to cover the attorney's fees, she'd rather pull her own weight. The money she'd received from Sam made that possible. "Consider it my contribution toward Sugar Sand Inn."

"But Reggie…" Michelle started. Her eyes widened.

"I know it isn't a lot. But it's all I have."

"It's not that," Michelle protested. "It's, well, it's very generous. But don't you want to hang on to some of it?"

"No," she said simply. As far as she was

concerned, the matter wasn't open for discussion. "I don't want a dime of Sam's money." She might have murky doubts about some things, but this was one thing that was perfectly clear.

When Michelle turned a questioning glance on Erin and Nina, they nodded in agreement with Reggie's decision.

"Okay, then," Michelle acquiesced. She slipped the envelope into a pocket. "This will come in handy, I'm sure." She lifted her glass. "Here's to us, the owners and proprietors of the soon-to-be-open Sugar Sand Inn."

Ice cubes rattled and glasses clinked as Reggie and the others raised their drinks in a toast. The conversation quickly shifted to their plans for the coming week. Nina had placed an ad for kitchen help in the local newspaper. Though the café wouldn't open for several months yet, she thought it might take some time to find just the right second-in-command. Michelle had begun prepping a couple of the upstairs rooms for guests and was excited about a shipment of comforters and linens that were due to arrive soon. Erin had spent the week visiting local tourist spots and reported that, though kayak rentals were plentiful nearby, no one provided the kind of guided tours the inn would offer. She planned to make a quick trip to the Keys to retrieve her own watercraft and asked if Reggie would go with her.

"The tomatoes are in bloom, and the beans won't be ready to pick for several more weeks. So sure. I can take a few days away from the garden." Lately, it had occupied most of her time. She would have said more, but a long, dark sedan coming up the driveway distracted her. "Who's that?" she asked.

"Not a clue," Michelle answered.

Curious, they all watched as the car rolled to a stop in front of the house. A tall, well-built man emerged from the vehicle. As he stepped into sight, Nina gasped. Mr. Pibbs, who'd been enjoying his nightly petting session, let out a yowl and sprang from her lap. In a flash, the cat disappeared through the open front door.

"What's wrong?" Reggie swung toward Nina.

Her skin an unhealthy ashen color, the chef only stared at the stranger.

Thank you for reading
*The Secret At Sugar Sand Inn*!

If you loved this book and want to help the
series continue,
take a moment to leave a review!

Want to know what happens next in
Sugar Sand Beach?

Sign up for Leigh's newsletter
to get the latest news about upcoming releases,
excerpts, and more!
https://leighduncan.com/newsletter/

# Books by Leigh Duncan

SUGAR SAND BEACH SERIES

The Gift at Sugar Sand Inn
The Secret at Sugar Sand Inn
The Cafe at Sugar Sand Inn
The Reunion at Sugar Sand Inn
Christmas at Sugar Sand Inn

HEART'S LANDING SERIES

A Simple Wedding
A Cottage Wedding
A Waterfront Wedding

ORANGE BLOSSOM SERIES

Butterfly Kisses
Sweet Dreams

HOMETOWN HEROES SERIES

Luke
Brett
Dan
Travis
Colt
Garrett
The Hometown Heroes Collection, A Boxed Set

LEIGH DUNCAN

SINGLE TITLE BOOKS

A Country Wedding
Journey Back to Christmas
The Growing Season
Pattern of Deceit
Rodeo Daughter
His Favorite Cowgirl

NOVELLAS

The Billionaire's Convenient Secret
A Reason to Remember

Find all Leigh's books at:
leighduncan.com/books

# Acknowledgements

Every book takes a team effort.
I want to give special thanks to those who made
*The Secret at Sugar Sand Inn* possible.

Cover design
Chris Kridler at
Sky Diary Productions

House photo used in cover illustration
Taken by Jerrye and Roy Klotz via Wikipedia,
licensed under Creative Commons
(link: https://creativecommons.org/licenses/by-
sa/4.0/deed.en)

Editing Services
Chris Kridler at
Sky Diary Productions

Interior formatting
Amy Atwell and Team
Author E.M.S.

# About the Author

Leigh Duncan is the award-winning author of more than two dozen novels, novellas and short stories. Though she started writing fiction at the tender age of six, she didn't get serious about writing a novel until her 40th birthday, and she offers all would-be authors this piece of advice: Don't wait so long!

Leigh sold her first, full-length novel in 2010. In 2017, she was thrilled when Hallmark Publishing chose her as the lead author for their new line of romances and cozy mysteries. A National Readers' Choice Award winner, an Amazon best-selling author and recently named a National Best-Selling author by Publisher's Weekly, Leigh lives on Florida's East Coast where she writes women's fiction and sweet, contemporary romance with a dash of Southern sass.

Want to get in touch with Leigh? She loves to hear from readers and fans. Visit leighduncan.com to send her a note. Join Leigh on Facebook, and don't forget to sign up for her newsletter so you get the latest news about fun giveaways, special offers or her next book!

# About the Cover

The minute I came up with the idea of writing about four best friends who open a beach-side inn, I knew exactly which house I wanted to put on the covers of these books. With its gingerbread trim and Queen Anne-style architecture, the Wood/Spann house is easily one of the most beautiful homes I've ever seen. Built in 1895 by F.S. Wood, the house is a part of Troy, Alabama's College Street Historical District and is listed in the National Registry of Historic Places. Best of all, it belongs to a member of my very own family!

Aunt Betty, thank you so much for letting me feature your incredible home on the covers of the books in the Sugar Sand Beach series!

Printed in Great Britain
by Amazon

10536681R00181